BROKEN ANGEL

BROKEN ANGEL

AMANDA RYAN

TABLE OF CONTENTS

DEDICATIONS

For Eileen, Mabel, and Shirley Mickleborough, often referred to as 'The Three Sisters'. Whilst this may sound more like a rather splendid rock formation, than mother and aunties, it is indeed fitting for being the solid, strong founding stones of our family. They still endure, in our thoughts, always missed with affection. Mum Eileen remains as my sounding board, bedrock, and thought processor with our endless, imaginary conversations.

In memory of Frank, for shining brightly, a joyous force of positivity that lifted spirits and lit up a room.

To my dad Barry for passing on his dogged, conscientious spirit, and drive. This determination ensures that things once started, like this book, no matter the obstacles, are completed. There is usually, always a way. He taught that tough stuff is 'character-building,' and I am stronger and more resilient for it.

To my brother Nick for simply being warm-hearted, wonderful Nick and adding the adjective 'Nickish' to my vocabulary, and to my lovely, steadfast brother Duncan for his selfless strength, quiet fortitude and helping hands. My brothers are safe islands in any storm.

To Anna, for insightful wisdom and messages at midnight and to young Archie for sharing with me, the joy of writing. He is the 'King of full notebooks!'

To Terry for teaching that it is fine not to be fine, and that in every situation there is a choice and a reason to laugh and smile. Whenever I am in a muddle, I think of him.

To husband Greg, my Ace of Hearts who always comes up trumps whenever I doubt myself or need a sympathetic ear. My number one since school days, we can chat from sunrise to sundown and never run out of things to say. He is always there for me: my affirmation, anchor, and the smile I need to see.

To my children: Josh, Gabriella, Georgie, and Saskia for being 'special humans' who make my world a better, brighter, place. They are the 'rescue quad squad' for my technology blind spot struggles, saving me from randomly pressing every button or key! They have taught me so much, offered fresh, new insights and have kept me young in spirit and outlook. I believe that they have successfully 'manifested' a better me!

Put simply, it is never winter when they are around for these special people warm my heart on the iciest of days; I would be lost without them.

Bowie, our black Labrador, for wagging his tail when he sees me, his bottomless love, and for teasing me with his toys, believing I want them as much as he does! His contented snoring is the comforting soundtrack to chill time.

For every reader who finds a piece of themselves or a loved one within this book.

ACKNOWLEDGEMENTS

Some of my earliest memories take me back to a time when make-believe was 'real': cans of peas 'grew' in our vegetable garden, I raced my shadow across the lawn, and replenished my mother's empty perfume bottles with my own rose petal and water mulch. Play was inventive and resourceful: I picked out well known tunes on milk bottles filled with various levels of water that I giddily struck with a stick, and created my own pretty garden, planting 'flowers' made from colourful tissues, matchsticks, and straws. Indoors the make believe continued with a magic wand my father had made from a bent wire coat hanger covered in silver tinsel, and the 'two little dickey birds, Peter and Paul' (that were sticky tabs on my father's nails) that he told to 'fly away' and 'come back' by deftly swapping his fingers. During this period, I also cut squares of paper with round tipped scissors for tiny hands, to make my own books. The edges were usually wonky, and the sticky tape puckered, but the hours flew by making up stories and adding pictures that I had drawn with my first set of 'Crayola' wax crayons. I remember, even back then, thinking how wonderful it would be to have my own 'proper' published book and to be that grown-up person called an author. For all these years, my mother kept one of these little books. Sadly, she passed away shortly after the publication of my debut novel 'The Indigo Trail,' but she did at least get to see and hold it in her hands. She had always appreciated my imagination and creative thought, and believing she would like me to continue writing, I embarked upon the sequel 'Broken Angel' when my own world was broken and falling apart. During this time of grieving and reminiscing whilst still trying to move forward, Bowie, our black Labrador, instinctively knowing when my heart is heavy, never left my side. He is my shadow and unwitting helper when I write and my breathing comfort blanket.

Recognition and appreciation must also go to the many neurodivergent people who have taught me new things, and are still helping me to grow as a more enlightened and rounded person in my adult years. Sometimes they are strangers, but they have removed the blinkers, giving new perspectives and insights into different ways of thinking, all of equal worth. These lessons have inspired my storytelling, drawing upon personal experience that I hope gives my writing a voice with a clear message: society is stronger and richer for neurodiversity, and these individuals should be valued, seen, and heard.

Oprah Winfrey famously said, 'Surround yourself with only people who are going to lift you higher.' My husband Greg's unyielding support and belief in me has given 'Broken Angel' its wings. He is my 'go to' receptor for offloading, sounding out my ideas and inspiration whilst offering trustworthy judgement and opinion whenever I am unsure. His regular refills of tea and coffee, or even a cheeky cheese scone that suddenly appears by the keyboard along with a few encouraging words, are happy fuel whilst in the creative zone. He keeps me keeping on even on the bleakest and toughest days.

My children Josh, Gabriella, Georgie, and Saskia, whilst now grown up and carving out new beginnings and lives are always ready ears offering this baby boomer a broader and younger perspective. They help me to view my writing through their millennial and Gen Z eyes, giving me balance to keep my writing relevant and more in touch with the reader.

Their growing up years and journey into adulthood has helped to flesh-out the characters, highlighting the underdog's strength to win through, and how often the playground bully, switches sides on becoming a parent. Whatever, the trials and tribulations, during this time, my children's kindness, and integrity, never wavered, holding true to their core values and in 'Broken Angel', too, keeping a selfless promise of kindness brings the story to its conclusion.

These people are my magic wand: their smiles, laughter, conversations, and uplifting presence have enabled me to fill these pages. It would not have happened without them.

MEMORIAL AT THE 'LIGHTNING TREE'

Nobody ever really dies until the last person who remembers us has also gone. Nevertheless, time is fleeting and so are we. Whether a life is long or short, whatever the dramas, events and people that shaped its story, in the end, it boils down to a handful of memories and meaningful moments. That life eventually condenses to a feeling their name triggers, be it good or bad, until said for the very last time. It is just how it is unless we have left behind something lasting.

Since the late 1920s in the village of Great Snubington, an ancient oak stricken by lightning was one such monument to time. Known as the Lightning Tree it was a fascinating contradiction: both an ugly and stunning stitch in the village's historic tapestry. A staunch and upright reminder of the dastardly storm and killer curse that caused havoc in the village almost seven decades earlier, time had unpicked the ugly stitch and replaced it with one of spellbinding beauty: the skeletal giant became a natural wonder with many different faces and moods depending on the time of day or season. Tiggy, now approaching her 30th birthday, had never tired of its imperious and magical silhouette dominating the skyline, the magnificent shapes of bare, jagged branches of this solitary tree, like a lone warrior after the battle on her favourite landscape she called 'Home'.

Just by being there, the Lightning Tree highlighted the passage of time, teaching lessons on 'lost time' and how not to waste or take it for granted. However, to Arthur Ramsbottom and the families of 14 victims of the storm's curse, it was also a thief, robbing them of time with their loved ones, and their loved ones of time. However, the village had lived curse-free for two decades thanks to Tiggy's childhood life-changing Indigo Trail, and now the time felt safe and right to commemorate the lives of those lost.

The year is 1996: the first flip mobile phone is on sale, The Spice Girls are a force for female empowerment, and an optimistic, football-loving nation is singing about 'Three Lions on a Shirt'. In Great Snubington, the villagers flocked to the Lightning Tree where Arthur Ramsbottom, Tiggy's former neighbour and a village favourite outside of Heavenly Gardens, would perform the tribute born out of love and funded from his own pockets. It would finally settle old demons, bringing a new dawn of meaningful acceptance to the bereaved community. The occasion really mattered to him, and so it did to Tiggy, too; she would not have missed the ceremony and 'the great unveiling,' as they had trailed it, for the world. For Arthur, it felt like the culmination of a lifetime lived without his twin ever since the eve of their tenth birthday almost seventy years ago.

It was a fine, sultry day in early September, and a decent turnout had gathered at the tree. Relatives and friends of the 14 curse victims had come from near and far, including Sharon, the former mobile hairdresser. She had flown in from Benidorm. The loss of her twin Cherie to the curse, and its final victim, had driven Sharon overseas. Nobody had seen her for years, and nothing highlighted the passage of time more than Sharon's appearance here: the former party girl and dating addict, hiding her curves in her flowing kaftan, looked wrinkled like a prune from years of Spanish sun.

Only one person had opposed the commemoration: the former Alicia Duncan Forbes, now in her late fifties, and having recently remarried to become Mrs Alicia Gold. It was rumoured that the apt surname, along with the man's obvious Lamborghini wealth, had sealed the deal with the self-indulgent and entitled gold digger. Over the last twenty years she hadn't changed a bit apart from the disappearance of her chin's hairy 'beauty spot' that she boasted now lived in a 'rare moles' jar in Harley Street. As if! Alicia refused to be ordinary, and even her moles had to be exceptional. Despite her objections, however, Alicia could not keep away. Her 'FOMO' saw to that. She had to be a part of anything and everything going on in 'Snubs' as she called Great Snubington.

'You're fools if you think the curse is over,' boomed a voice. It was Alicia. She was an enormous wildebeest of a woman, a beast of nature, emboldened by moving in a pack, except with a predatory instinct.

The onlookers whispered, used to Alicia being centre stage of every village occasion. She craved attention, particularly from the media, and she was always the village's voice and focal point for general news articles; in fact, her many newspaper images decorated the walls of the village hall.

'Just look at me! I'm like a special edition, deluxe wallpaper!' she had boasted, pointing them out to any newcomer to set foot in the place.

The 'media savvy' Alicia Gold would somehow ensure she made the local newspaper's front-page headlines by hijacking the occasion to be all about her.

'I'm telling you now and I'll tell you again, Thomas Tipple was struck down by the curse,' she insisted. The villagers, stunned by her insensitivity, stared at his widow and children. Tiggy, the youngest Tipple family member, spat at the ground in disgust. It was not a good look, and she instantly regretted it, but she was seething.

Alicia ignored her, 'Death by lawn mower! That doesn't just happen without the intervention of a curse.'

Georgina Tipple sobbed, the deep wound of her husband's death beginning to weep again. Her eldest daughter, Penelope, put her arm around her mother as her fiancé, Adam Green, in turn, squeezed her hand.

Tiggy whispered to Arthur, 'It was no such thing!' but Alicia wouldn't stop.

'The curse is still as deadly today as it ever has been.'

The mumblings were clearly not on Alicia's side.

'You're counting your chickens! There'll be more victims,' she shouted as the press photographers snapped away.

Arthur retorted, 'And who are you—Chicken Little?'

Everyone laughed except for Alicia.

'What's Chicken Little?' asked a young girl with pigtails and freckles. Her name was Daisy Dingles. 'I can't see any chickens!'

'It's a story of a chicken that gets hit on the head by an acorn; it thinks the sky is falling in,' her mother shouted over the noise of the lively gathering.

'That doesn't make her a chicken!' Daisy said, staring at Alicia, who was waiting for her moment to fire back.

'Chicken Little!' Alicia scoffed, 'I never said the world is ending! Although it did for this lot,' she said callously, pointing to a stand of roses with each curse victim's name.

Daisy looked scared. 'The world is ending?'

'That curse will strike again; it's not if, but when.' Alicia stared at a woman in the front row for far too long, 'Who'll be next?' she asked, making the woman squirm. It was chilling.

Daisy whimpered, 'I want to go home!'

'Don't worry, sweetheart, nothing bad is going to happen,' her mother reassured her. 'We all know the curse is no longer a thing.'

'Old people say odd things,' Daisy concluded, looking Alicia up and down, her eyes settling upon the woman's extra-large feet that appeared even longer in her flat Mary Janes.

Arthur Ramsbottom hobbled forward, steadying himself with his stick in front of a wooden plinth draped with a cloth.

'As many of you already know, I lost my twin brother, Arnold, to a terrible storm,' Arthur began. 'It was almost seventy years ago on the eve of our 10th birthday, and yet it still feels like only yesterday,' he continued, 'this very special, ancient oak, marks the spot that I last saw my kind and funny, wonderful twin.' Arthur pointed his stick heavenward, following the tree's scarred and twisted branches, pausing to reflect. The tree was, in a way, also a victim of the storm.

Daisy Dingles was keen to fill the pause, 'What's special about it?' she asked, swinging her sun-bleached pigtails behind her and folding her arms. 'It's just a tree, a silly, ugly tree!' She looked cross as she stuck out her tongue at the oak's cracked trunk.

Daisy's mother raised a finger to her lips to silence her. Dave Dodds, the curse's penultimate victim, was Daisy's uncle, and this explained her indignation. She had never known her uncle, but the tree was still standing, a survivor despite the curse.

Arthur continued, 'I used to feel like that, Daisy, but over the years, my anger for this tree has changed to respect. I see it now as our Lightning Tree and a symbol of strength and resilience, a wake-up call from the universe of a higher power.' Arthur and Tiggy's eyes met, knowing that only they both understood the meaning of this higher power: it was the 'Wobniar,' the Guardian of the Rainbow, Arthur's lost twin, Arnold. Tiggy's Indigo Trail adventures had taught her that.

'I, therefore, feel it is only fitting that we remember our loved ones in this place with a lasting memorial. They should never be forgotten,' Arthur said.

Emotions were building in the crowd with tearful hugs and squeezes until a young boy called Theo lifted the sombre energy. His older brother was Penelope Tipple's fiancé, Adam.

'Lightning is an electrical discharge caused by imbalances between storm clouds and the ground or within the cloud themselves,' Theo announced.

'Button it! Einstein!' Alicia snapped, 'Who needs to know that!'

She stomped over to him, sneering, and brandishing an egg in a manner best described as threatening.

Theo had lots more to say; he was a wealth of scientific information and had a gem or two for every situation.

'Not now, Theo!' Adam whispered into his little brother's ear.

Arthur read out the curse victims full names, everyone clapping as each relative took their rose from the stand and laid it at the base of the Lightning Tree. Arthur's big moment had finally arrived, the photographers with their large lenses surrounding him to capture the unveiling.

'Now to permanently commemorate those lives on the 20th anniversary of the curse being lifted…' Arthur announced, taking hold of the cloth for the big reveal.

'You're counting your chickens!' Alicia Gold heckled, but all eyes were on Arthur as he removed the sheet, revealing a beautiful hand-carved acorn, crafted from one of the Lightning Tree's fallen boughs: the acorn's cupule displaying the engraved names of every curse victim in honour of a life taken too soon.

'Here's your acorn, Chicken Little!' Arthur mocked, pointing to the beautiful, wooden carving. He looked Alicia in the eye, 'Your curse is no more a thing than 'The sky is falling in', Chicken Little!'

Arthur clucked, flapping his arms, prompting others to join in, overpowering Alicia's response. The journalists were jotting down notes as the photographers captured this exciting twist on the commemoration story. However, Alicia, fuming and feeling humiliated, was determined to have the last word, and switching to 'Power play' mode, threw her egg to splatter upon the lens of the nearest camera.

Chapter 2

WEDDING SURPRISES

'When life gives you lemons, make lemonade.' Tiggy lived by this philosophy, and with the 'big 3 zero' looming, she had, certainly in the romance stakes, dated a fruit bowl's worth of absolute lemons. Nevertheless, in her strong and positive mind, it was all champagne and roses, never dwelling on the sour taste that the bad lemons had left behind. She had always made the most of the lemonade's fizz until it went flat and cloudy.

Twenty years on from Tiggy's rainbow exploits changing her world and lifting the village's curse, Tiggy's string of failed romances contrasted with her older sister

Penelope's seamless success in finding the love of her life. The sisters had been a united force of 'girl power' energy, living together in the old farmhouse, now updated with blonde wood, chintz soft furnishings, and bean bags for cosy time in front of the television and video player. The farmhouse, surrounding land, and everything Mrs Derbyshire owned, she had gifted to her 'adopted family' when she, their dear Mrs 'D' had left this earth. It was the impetus for Tiggy's BMX training academy and Penelope's drop-in recreational hub, 'Every Child Matters', to exist.

'Every Child Matters' was Penelope and fiancé Adam's vision they brought to life in a converted barn. Penelope had hung up her dancing shoes, the time feeling right to settle down and pass on her skills. Penelope locked the door to 'Every Child Matters', checking it twice. She checked everything twice to keep her late father's memory alive. Thomas Tipple was a risk-limiting-belt-and-braces-man.

A smartly dressed woman with a document folder under one arm and a bulging carrier bag of groceries was striding out towards her. She looked frazzled: flushed, harassed, and rushing at the end of a busy day. Her teenage son, Solomon, cowered behind her, shrinking to hide beneath his afro. He was a gentle soul, his rich brown eyes transfixed on Penelope's feet. Solomon liked Penelope, but nobody would have known.

'Solomon has something for you, haven't you, Solomon?' his mother said, giving him a gentle nudge.

The women's smiles exchanged an ocean of understanding. He was clutching a white rose that was hanging by his knees. Solomon neither spoke nor raised his head or the flower, Penelope tentatively putting her hand onto the rose's stem for Solomon to loosen his grip.

'Thank you, Solomon. It's beautiful!' Penelope said, smiling, wishing he would look at her, but knowing that he wouldn't.

'There would have been no sleep for either of us until it had been delivered,' the woman said, tugging on her son's sleeve. 'Let's get you home and get some supper on,' and without a glance, Solomon and his mother had gone.

Penelope put the rose to her nose, reading a label trailing from the stem:

'If teachers were flowers, I would pick you.'

This was everything.

✿✿✿✿✿✿✿✿✿✿✿✿

As housemates, Penelope and Tiggy sometimes squabbled, but they were tight. When Tiggy's relationships crumbled, Penelope picked up the pieces, regardless of where she was performing or Tiggy was competing. Life had been hectic, but they were close and cosy home birds, always flocking together, enjoying their 'sister time' despite their in-house joke of 'Tiggyness:' things like Tiggy's trainers' muddy trails everywhere, fishing maggots in the fridge, (the boyfriend's, not hers) her awful round-the-clock singing, and drinking orange juice straight from the carton. Penelope was tolerant, often sharing the sofa with Tiggy's 'bad boy lemons.' In contrast, it had happily been Penelope and Adam for years, and now they were getting married.

Georgina breathed in the scent of Solomon's white rose in her old cut crystal bud vase on the top of the television and sighed, 'Poor Alex! He hates that he can't be here, but your brother's sent you a message.'

Her daughters were laying out their dresses and accessories for the big day. Georgina checked her watch before pressing the 'play' button on the video recorder; Alex flashed onto the screen from an office full of desktop computers, clever-looking colleagues, and the Stars 'n' Stripes flag in the background.

'Hi Pen! Sowwy I can't be with you on your special day. I'm working 24/7 on the Delta Launch. I know you'll look the perfect bwide and Adam is a vewy lucky man! Have a bwilliant time and make sure you keep Mum off the shewwy! Sending you more love than all the stars in the galaxies!'

'I miss him!' Penelope sighed, admiring the twinkling sequin embroidery on her veil.

'Alex is still nuts about David Bowie; you'd be walking up the aisle to 'Love you 'til Tuesday.' It's hardly 'til death us do part!' Tiggy joked, taking the veil and gazing through the tulle. 'A bit fancy, sis! Not bad for a Heavenly Gardens reject!'

They dissolved into fits of giggles, enjoying this special moment. There had been little laughter since Thomas Tipple, husband and father, had died, or as Alex said at the funeral, 'put out the lights and left Planet Earth for the celestial good'. The family missed his strength and funny ways whether he was, in his words, 'jobbing a job' or cruising the roads as a demon biker. It was unbelievable to think that he was gone.

'Who's that?' Penelope asked, startled by an over-enthusiastic knock at the door. Buddy, the black Labrador, ambled over to it, barking like the guard dog he most certainly wasn't.

'I'll go!' Georgina said, running her fingers across the silky fabric of her daughter's dress and stepping over some wedding presents blocking her way. She was grinning as if she were in on a secret.

'Surpwise!' The girls' faces lit up. Only one person they knew spoke like that. Alex still had the distinction of not rolling his 'r's.

Their brother burst in, dropped his heavy suitcase, narrowly missing his sisters' toes, and wrapped his arms around them like a grinning gorilla. Alex was tall, dark, and slim like his late father and looked like a brain box with or without his glasses. The apple had not fallen far from the tree. As a boy, Alex was often told he had his 'head in the clouds', but now, in his early thirties, he had surpassed it: his head was well and truly stuck in space, a rocket scientist for NASA living out his childhood dream.

'Did you weally think I'd miss my oldest sis'getting hitched?' Alex quipped. 'I pwomised to give you away, Pen. I'll job that job for Father. By the way,' he added, still squeezing his sisters breathless, not wanting to let go, 'The Bitch Queen' is on the warpath.'

'Alicia?' Georgina asked, looking filled with dread.

Alex nodded. 'There was also a young guy hanging awound, wearwing a bucket hat and acid wash jeans. He didn't look like one of hers,' he said, releasing his sisters to comfort their mother.

'I think I've seen him about recently. He asked for 'jelly' in the shop. He was shocked it wasn't in a jar!' Georgina said with a smirk.

'Can't that wretched woman just leave us alone for once?' Penelope mumbled. 'She says the children are a risk to the community. She's ridiculous!'

'Wemedials wunning wampant, apparwently!' Alex scoffed.

'Psycho!' Tiggy murmured.

'Sowwy I'm not awound to support you,' Alex said, stroking Buddy who was nuzzling his head against him. Everyone had missed Alex, Buddy included.

'NASA and the Milky Way need our rocket crazy sib,' Penelope said, and everyone laughed. They would have laughed at anything, just happy being together once more. 'Besides, you've been more than generous with your cheque book, buying us the therapy animals,' Penelope said, giving him a consoling peck on the cheek.

Georgina was mentally 'gone'. Alicia was all she could think about, anxiously peering out of the window, 'If that ghastly woman ruins the day...' she said, drawing the blind.

'She'll try,' Tiggy responded, 'she's never forgiven us for turning our backs on Heavenly Gardens.'

'And we can't stop them. They've discovered a public right of way on our land,' Georgina said. She looked resigned.

'How insufferwable!' Alex added, 'twenty years and still bearwing a gwudge, but like they matter. We'll still have a blast! Stick the kettle on! I could murder a pwoper bwew!'

Chapter 3

THE WEDDING AND THE PROTEST

The next day, as predicted, Alicia was out to cause trouble; she was still just as garish and flash with her jewellery and her oversized flipper feet certainly hadn't shrunk. The irritating, imperious woman was outside the church gates waiting for the bride to arrive and clicking her fingers, her Heavenly Gardens disciples surrounded her with placards and megaphones. Alicia's newest recruit, a curvy, body-confident woman and 'Take That' super fan called 'Rach', had joined the protesters for the first time.

'Watch out for any on the loose! They could be dangerous,' Alicia instructed.

Rach looked confused, 'But aren't they children?' she asked, fiddling with the black rose pinned to her tight-fitting, low-cut 'Take That' t-shirt. Rach had worn a black rose ever since the band had broken up earlier in the year.

'Weird children,' Alicia asserted, 'weird and wild.'

'Agreed!' Gertie Grimshaw mumbled from her wheelchair, cradling her favourite gnome. The childless woman was still gnome obsessed.

'Timothy, push me where I can see,' she snapped, 'I want to see the action!'

'Don't you want to see the bride, dear?' her husband responded.

'I've seen enough brides to last me a lifetime. We just want them shut down,' she grumbled.

'They will be!' Alicia reassured her.

Alicia was a force of self-interest, and only those useful to her were friends or, with brag-worthy credentials, made 'husband material'. She was, by third-party association, powerful and protected.

From opening its doors on the very first day, Every Child Matters (ECM to the locals) was on Alicia's

'Banish List'. Adam Green, the founder, wanted a place for his little brother, Theo, to be happy. School was a daily dread. Theo struggled to fit in; people overlooked and misunderstood him, so it was hardly surprising if he withdrew or lashed out. It was a vicious circle with everyone confused. Theo just wanted to be accepted, but instead, he was troubled, disconnected from the world, and not given a chance. It was unnecessarily sad. Alicia certainly did not understand, and in her words, Every Child Matters was 'nothing but a plague on their prestigious postcode'.

A young mixed-race man wearing a bucket hat and melting smile rocked up, 'Is this the Tipple's wedding?' he enquired, pocketing some keys to a retro Volkswagen campervan he had just parked at the roadside.

Alicia glared, 'It's a protest! Can't you see!' she snapped, waving her placard in a hostile fashion.

'I think I'll hang around for a bit if nobody minds,' he said, not bothered and locking eyes with Rach, who couldn't take her eyes off him.

'Who's he?' Rach enquired, watching him walk away, his red holdall slung across the shoulder of his baseball jacket, taking up a prime viewing spot by the porch entrance. The stranger wasn't typical for these parts: he was confident and oozed charisma. 'What a dish!' she said, flicking her hair extensions.

'No idea. He's like a rotten smell that keeps hanging around. Honestly, Rach, you and your over-active hormones!' Alicia replied, clicking her fingers for her attention, wanting to get the protest underway.

'What do we want?' Alicia yelled through her loudspeaker.

'Shut down!'

'When do we want it?'

'Now!' her entourage responded.

The bridal party and guests ignored them. They were looking sharp to celebrate in style: tailcoats, cravats, floral buttonholes, and statement hats topped off by big smiles. Even Nureyev, Penelope and Adams' pet greyhound was wearing a white bowtie. Tiggy was turning heads as Maid of Honour in her floor-length gown, a sight previously unseen, whilst Penelope was a breathtaking vision of romantic elegance. The dancer in her was obvious, whether it was her supreme poise, gliding down the aisle despite her heavy train and teetering high heels, or maybe her slender swan-like neck and sculpted high cheekbones, Penelope was the most regal of brides, as if she had always been born for this moment.

Alicia stepped up the protest outside, 'Every Child Matters, shut down now!' she shouted. 'Who matters?'

'We do!' her 'faithfuls' responded, drowning out the exchange of vows inside the church.

Fortunately, the happy couple only had eyes and ears for each other. Alicia and her mob were wasting their breath and their time. Suddenly, some of the youngsters from Every Child Matters, in the back pews, appeared outside the church, forming a 'Guard of Honour'.

'SHOO!' Alicia shrieked, waving her placard at one of the girls to move out of her way.

'You've got big feet, I've got little feet, but you can have it,' the sweet girl responded, taking off a shoe and offering it to Alicia.

'Rude! Who does she think she is?' Alicia snarled. 'I said SHOO!'

The girl looked confused, removing her other shoe.

'I'm Daisy Dingles,' she said, holding out both shoes.

Alicia scowled and, turning her back, muttered, 'Stupid creature!'

Solomon had watched the entire episode, staring at Alicia with a burning intensity that was unnerving. He could not take his eyes off her.

It stopped Alicia in her tracks, and as she stared back at him, she shuddered, 'Dunno what you're gawping at but stop it!'

Solomon ignored her and continued to stare. He was a still and silent penetrating presence amidst the noisy activity. It was 'his terms, his world'. Alicia glared.

'Normal!' she said in a deeply sarcastic tone, meaning the opposite. 'Follow me!' she ordered, and as her mob dutifully headed off to continue their protest, Alicia couldn't help but look back over her shoulder to see if he was still staring at her. He was. Solomon hadn't flinched an inch.

✿✿✿✿✿✿✿✿✿✿✿✿

The reception was on the Tipple's farmland. The lemon and white striped marquee stood resplendent: the fine billowing canvas with its silky draped interior served as the perfect backdrop for the celebrations. It was a piece of home, yet lavished with abundant festoons of lilies, daisies, and roses, whilst balloons and streaming ribbons floated up from every table. A romantic haven of love celebrated beneath one roof: fresh, simple styling wrapped up in such a warm ambience, the mood inside the tent felt like sunshine in a jar.

The conversation and wine flowed, the guests drowning out the protesters outside, smugly camped out on a recently unearthed footpath and public right of way. It had been a masterstroke of Hugo Uppingham, Alicia's sidekick, the community know-it-all and retired legal eagle. He had ferreted through files and files of council documents and ordnance survey maps and had found everything they needed to make the Tipples' lives difficult.

ECM had their own table with a big tub of Lego to keep things calm. Alex banged his fist hard and loudly on the head table, shaking out the pain beneath the tablecloth, hoping nobody had noticed. Theo covered his sensitive ears to the noise and started to rock.

'Perhaps Theo and his friends should be on another table?' Penelope whispered to Adam, watching Theo disappear with a handful of Lego bricks beneath a long tablecloth. Apart from the muted protest a distance away, the guests were silent, waiting for Alex to speak on behalf of his late father.

Alex glanced at his bullet points scribbled onto his napkin, *Men are fwom Mars, Women are fwom Venus,* wote John Gway,' he began. 'In my opinion, Pen, you're a match for the beautiful goddess Venus.'

'Is he Adonis?' called out Theo's friend Simon, pointing with a Rubik's cube at the groom.

'Sort of,' Alex smiled.

Simon began mumbling Shakespeare's narrative poem Venus and Adonis. It was 1,194 lines in length, and Simon knew them all. He was still staring at his cube.

Suddenly, Theo poked his head out from beneath the table, 'Venus is the hottest planet. It spins clockwise on its axis,' he said. Simon stared at him and nodded, the two friends knowing that they were about to go head-to-head in the battle of the Venuses, the planet versus the goddess.

'Cowect!' Alex agreed before getting his speech back on track. 'For thirty-one years I have been lucky enough to have Penelope, my dear pwecious sister, in my life. We have played, laughed, cwied, dweamed, and gwown up together.'

'It rains sulphuric acid,' Theo interrupted.

Alex continued, 'and thwough it all, you have always spwead love and beauty in everwything you do and today as Adam's bwide, so wadiant in white, you are twuly an absolute vision.' Penelope blushed.

'Here, here!' Arthur Ramsbottom called out, 'Beautiful inside and out!'

'It's an iambic pentameter quatrain and couplet,' Simon countered, unaware of some sniggers at the back of the marquee.

'It has an iron core but no magnetic field,' Theo mumbled, sitting back on his chair again.

Adam gestured for him to hush as Alex battled on, 'I am so pwoud to call you my sister, and I know that if our dear father were here today,' Alex said, holding strong, 'he'd echo these words about his incwedible daughter that he loved so vewy dearly.'

Georgina Tipple dabbed her eyes with her napkin. She had known that today would be emotional. Suddenly, the protest chants from outside became louder, and the eyes of the guests flickered to the marquee's entrance, wondering if there was to be an invasion.

All this time, Solomon, seated opposite to Theo, had been quietly drawing, completely in a world of his own. He took his sketchpad and pencil case everywhere, and although he hadn't seemed aware that Alex was even speaking, he had reproduced Botticelli's famous masterpiece of the goddess of love and beauty spawned from the giant scallop shell. It was remarkable.

'Our father will be looking down, happy that Adam, the young man he met and welcomed into the family all those years ago, is now your husband, Pen.' Adam smiled, but there were moist eyes all around; Thomas Tipple's passing had been a sudden and seismic shock to the community. Alex continued, 'He thought of you as a son, Adam, and that you and Pen were a perfect match. There can be no doubt that you're making a positive differwence to so many young lives. As family, fwiends, and villagers, we should be so pwoud of that.'

'What do we want?' the protesters shouted. The guests looked concerned.

'Ignore the wabble!' Alex retaliated, giving it the thumbs down to huge applause.

'A day on Venus is longer than a year; it hardly rotates at all,' Theo called out, still not done.

'Twue again!' Alex responded, 'I can see I need to put in a good word for you at NASA!'

The marquee bubbled over with laughter, and the atmosphere was light and frothy once more.

'So, if we can waise our glasses to toast our happy couple, 'To Penelope and Adam!'

Chapter 4

TODD

The stranger in the bucket hat's name was Todd. His appearance at the Tipple's wedding had caused waves of suspicion, talked about across the counter and amongst the newspaper stands and sweet jars in Great Snubington's village shop. The consensus was that the young man seemed too invested in the wedding to be a mere stranger or casual bystander; he had taken photographs and thrown confetti outside the church, and yet nobody knew him. Alicia Gold had spread the malicious rumour that he might be the late Thomas Tipple's love child, wanting to see his half-sister getting married. Alicia revelled in spawning toxic gossip and creating unhappiness wherever she could. That said, it was one-way traffic with the wedding party; it was as if he knew them, but they had no inkling of who he was or how he came to be there. This was another story entirely. His bulky red holdall was hiding the truth; he took it everywhere and guarded it as if it were as important as life itself. It was.

Monday to Friday, Todd was a city slicker, suited, booted, and looking sharp except for the holdall that had a lived-in appearance from constant use. It was the Thursday after the wedding, and at the end of an ordinary day at work, Todd was preparing to clock off. He tipped some dregs of cold coffee down the office kitchen's sink, tidied his desktop, put his four-leafed clover paperweight into his holdall, and was then, in Todd's words, 'Another day, another dollar, outta here.'

Todd walked to his campervan a distance away, passing his favourite ice cream parlour and fast food restaurant, calling in to eat and for a washroom stop before the drive home. The truth is that Todd had no home, only his campervan that he parked off-road in a different spot each evening. It was the same daily routine: Todd went in as 'Smart Todd' in the suit and came out as 'Casual Todd' in his baseball shirt and jeans. Every evening, the same transformation took place, predictable and unremarkable.

Casual Todd came out of the restaurant, headphones on, walking to the rhythm of his Walkman and onto the pedestrian crossing. He did not hear the approaching vehicle that knocked him off his feet, bouncing him off its bonnet, throwing him clear of the crossing and sending his holdall flying to land several metres away. The driver didn't stop, the vehicle gone in a flash. Todd was lying at the roadside, dazed but conscious and shaken up. Yet Todd's mind was not on himself or the hit-and-run driver: all he could think about was his holdall.

Todd had arrived in the UK in the spring of that year, travelling around in his campervan, looking to settle when he had found the reason for his being there. An 'all-American beefcake,' he was a newcomer to the island: a couple of failed relationships down the track, he was looking for a fresh start, and to rekindle some magic from his youth by finding the person that had left a handprint on his heart. It would be usual for his memory of the girl he had met in his early teens to by now be like a faded photograph, but her light still burned as brightly today as it had many years before. Who would have thought that an American with an obsession for baseball, peanut butter, and jelly would only finally feel he had found his happy place once discovering the small, sleepy village of Great Snubington? It did not seem a fit at all.

Todd clutched his holdall like a mother clinging onto a baby she thought she had lost but had then found, never wanting to let it out of her sight ever again.

'Are you OK?' he said, staring into the bag, and after a few seconds, he looked relieved. 'Frickin' freaky!' he mumbled, zipping up the bag again. 'Can't believe that just happened and you've winked at me!'

Todd looked up at the sky, losing his head in its clouds. The impact of the accident had agitated a jumble of buried memories, not all of them good. Todd had an unusual past, and some of it had resurfaced, breaking through into his consciousness from a time that he had kept locked away. He held his head, desperate to smother the haunting dark thought invaders. The truth is, Todd was a failed Rainbow Child, and the scars had reopened.

That night, when Todd was sleeping in his campervan, the night terrors returned with vengeance, forcing him back into the darkness of the rainbow's Indigo Realm, the home of all negative energy. Todd yelled out as his past replayed in his sleep: a lone figure at the mercy of the terrifying Dreamstealers once more. These hideous, black-feathered angels with huge skulls and black hearts were a part of Todd's story that he wanted to forget. Todd tossed and turned, tangling the sheets to escape his imagined enemy. He could still smell the rotting stench of the realm's negative energy as he buried himself into his pillow to muffle his dream's senses. If only he could have ended the story there, but to be unconscious is to lose control, and the Realm's Ogidni, a deadly seven-headed serpent, was about to attack. Todd thrashed around beneath his covers, a sleeping warrior, shielding himself, protecting his face as he relived the moment that the Ogidni had struck. It wasn't real, but every fibre of his being felt that it was. Todd punched his pillow to survive. The Ogidni was poised to strike again, but at its terrifying climax, Todd awoke to find his pyjamas soaked in sweat. For the rest of the night, he stayed awake, fearful the nightmare might return. The torment of the Indigo Realm had been such a long time ago, but suddenly his past was his present again, and something he needed to settle so as not to be a hostage to fear.

Chapter 5

BMX MANIA

'BMX Mania' had opened two years earlier on the late Mrs Derbyshire's gifted farmland. This was Tiggy's dream factory, making future stars of the track. Mrs 'D' never saw the track's completion, but the farmer's widow had cried happy tears when Tiggy raced her way to glory to become world champion. In her teens, Tiggy dominated the sport, her rivals wanting to crush the girl from Great Snubington, known worldwide in BMX circles as 'The Invincible One'.

'Pump harder!' Tiggy yelled, watching a tight pack of helmeted juniors pounding the pedals of their BMXs. These were her Advanced Juniors who she had trained from scratch.

'Great cornering!' she called out, unaware that Rach and her daughter were hovering to have a word. 'Finish hard........harder!' she shouted, while stroking Buddy, her old faithful, sat obediently waiting for the session to finish for his 'good boy' treats.

The huge rivalry between the children was always bubbling beneath the surface, the confident pack giving it everything to cross the line first. A little lad with flames on his helmet, fist pumped the air in victory.

'Save it for the next comp,' Tiggy shouted, 'I've told you, we're a squad, MJ, 'All for one and one for all!'

'Gotcha, Tigs!' the boy replied, saluting her.

'Less cheek!' Tiggy said, but inwardly grinning.

'All for one and one for all!' Michaela, a small, runny-nosed girl, repeated.

Michaela and Mikey Junior were twins and, whilst alike and inseparable, they were fiercely competitive with each other. Known as MJ and Micky at the academy, they boasted that one day they would be more famous in the village than both Michael Jackson and Mickey Mouse. It annoyed the competent but less able riders, and Sid, Tyler, and Jaden, amongst the boys, dreamed of the day that they could 'wipe that smug smile off his face,' meaning MJ. Along with Corey, Luca, and Ed, they called themselves 'The Lads', a label that quickly stuck. The competitive tension always simmered, and Micky, in a class of her own amongst the girls, faced the brunt of it. Suki and Megan were her closest rivals, but they ganged up with the next best riders, Laura, Ebony, and Beth. They had copied 'The Lads', calling themselves 'The Girls', freezing out Micky and excluding her from their chats and sleepovers to make themselves feel better. They were decent riders, and if Micky wasn't around, they would be vying for top spot. It irked them that they could never beat her. Those that, to be brutally honest, made up the numbers and were not top contenders had a foot in each camp. Tiggy privately thought of them as 'The Swiss' and whilst they were unlikely to dazzle on the track, she was grateful for their neutrality.

'Three final straight sprints to finish; and it's for the gold!' Tiggy called out, suddenly noticing Rach and her daughter. 'Two ticks and I'll be with you.'

Tiggy glanced back at the pack on the track. This was home where she knew she belonged, and ended each day counting her blessings from the Indigo Trail. It was buzzing with activity as the next session's advanced seniors warmed up, and a constant flow of parents were dropping off and picking up.

'Same time tomorrow!' she said high fiving 'The Swiss', and each later rider as they passed her on their way out.

'Gold medal cornering, you two,' Tiggy whispered to Mikey Junior and Michaela.

'Bo would like to start,' Rach said, thrusting her daughter in front of her like a prize protégé. 'Her friend Izzy comes on Tuesdays?'

Buddy wandered over, hoping they might have a treat, and began sniffing their legs.

'Gotta bike?' Tiggy asked, zoning in on Rach's Mrs Mark Owen sweatshirt.

Bo looked at her mum. Rach shook her head.

'No worries. We've spares,' Tiggy said, pointing to a rack of bikes of all sizes. 'Try before you buy! It's not for everyone.'

'She wants to be a 'biker babe boy magnet' like Izzy,' Rach added, unaware of Bo stroking Buddy to hide her embarrassment.

'Stay and watch the seniors, all of them novices less than two years ago,' Tiggy said like a proud parent. 'Feel free to browse the office,' Tiggy pointed to the old but refurbished windmill. 'You'll see the club photos and boards.' Her eyes flashed back to Rach's pink top again. 'What's your full name, kiddo? I'm guessing it's not Bo Owen!'

Rach laughed, 'I'm working on it!'

'I've a Beginners' group, Wednesday at 4.'

Bo's face dropped, 'But Izzy...'

'Izzy's in the intermediates,' Tiggy interjected, 'work hard and I'll soon move you up. That's how it works.'

Bo nodded. Tiggy did not negotiate. 'Seniors! Three laps of the track. No bumping!' Tiggy called out.

She noticed that Mikey Junior and Michaela were still there.

'It's morphin' time!' Mikey Junior shouted, pretending to be a Power Ranger.

'Is it Mum or Dad fetching you today?' Tiggy asked.

The other children had long since gone, but as usual, the twins were still waiting. They looked blank but, Tiggy didn't mind; the twins ticked boxes—skilful, daring, dogged, and competitive. They had the calibre to be champions.

The old windmill, Tiggy's favourite childhood haunt, had undergone major changes. These days it was multi-functioning: an office, a safe space, first aid hub, and a thriving BMX Academy's headquarters. Nevertheless, one of Tiggy's childhood chalk drawings remained: Tiggy wearing a gold medal and standing on the rostrum. It had been a successful manifestation: the club walls lined with cabinets gleaming with her trophies and medals collected from years of racing and winning.

'There's Izzy!' Bo said pointing at a newspaper cutting pinned to the Academy's 'News Board'.

'What's that?' Rach muttered, hearing a noise outside and peering out of the slightly open door.

Alicia Gold was heading towards them with a sealed envelope, singing along to her Sony Walkman, her massive size 11 feet flattening the grass with purpose.

'It's Alicia!' Rach whispered, panicked that Alicia might find her on enemy soil. 'Hide!' she ordered, pulling Bo inside the 'first aid and other stuff' cupboard. 'Alicia will be livid if she finds us here.'

Rach and Bo held their breath, frozen and silent, dreading what might happen next. Alicia stepped inside, put the envelope on the office desk, and then left as quickly as she had arrived.

Back at the track, Tiggy was completely unaware of Alicia's visit, the twins' father, Mikey, having eventually turned up.

'They'll have to miss for a bit. I'm on lates,' Mikey said, gesturing to the twins to get into the car.

'Can't their Mum do it?' Tiggy asked, 'I'll soon be selecting my competition squad for the UK's next year.'

Mikey shrugged. High school sweethearts, Mikey and Sapphire, had grown up and split up and were now at war with each other.

'They're talented, but it needs commitment,' Tiggy urged, sensing their championship prospects were slipping through her fingers.

'The ex barely leaves the gaff for the twins since she's got the sprog.'

'Hard work beats talent when talent doesn't work hard. I need them here.'

Tiggy was battling for them. She knew how much they wanted it.

'Please, Dad!' Michaela pleaded, wiping her runny nose with her sleeve.

Her brother pitched in, too. 'We want to be in the squad!'

'I'll have a word,' Mikey agreed.

Chapter 6

HEAVENLY GARDENS

'Look at this!' Tiggy said, thrusting a letter under her mother's nose.

Georgina Tipple had dropped by hoping for a relaxed wedding debrief: who wore what, who said what to whom, and who had drunk too much. There had been so much excited anticipation that now the wedding was over, things felt flat, and Georgina just wanted to relive it beyond finding stray pieces of confetti everywhere. Besides, Adam's Auntie Bren' had had too much wine and wore a huge bright yellow feathery hat that was so 'out there' that it was one of the wedding's main talking points.

Georgina sank into the grey furry bean bags, grabbing for her glasses as Buddy slumped down by her feet.

'It was in the office when I'd finished classes,' Tiggy explained as her mother read the letter written in Alicia's flamboyant hand. 'It's Alicia spreading her poison, wanting to close us down.'

Her mother pursed her lips. 'She's certainly determined,' Georgina concluded, passing it back, 'Contacting our local MP, petitioning, and lobbying Parliament. Goodness me!'

'It's nasty!' Tiggy said, looking upset. Her eyes were moist, 'I just don't understand it.' Her bottom lip quivered, and then a tear trickled down her face.

Georgina stared. 'Is this about Alicia, or are you still upset about Gavin?' Georgina asked, passing her daughter the box of tissues.

Tiggy's mouth gaped, 'I can't believe you just said that! I'm so over Gav. He wanted another chance, but I told him to shove it where the sun doesn't shine!'

'Good! Staying out all night, squandering money; he was never gonna be the one.'

'I know! You were right not to like him,' she said, drying her eyes. It was unusual for Tiggy, the tough, resilient 'invincible one', to let her walls down, but today they had tumbled.

'It'ud be nice though for you to meet that special someone.' Georgina was pushing her luck.

'Oh Mum! Can you not!' I've this one. He's enough!' Tiggy responded, stroking Buddy, who was at her side having sensed her upset.

'Now Penny has gone, you could have a housemate?' Georgina suggested, retreating a little but still handing her a flyer advertising a monthly local house-mating event in the nearby town. 'Anyway, what about that awful, yellow feathery hat? It had to be a bet!' Georgina joked to change the subject, 'I can't believe Glenda Harrington would design something so hideous. I thought she'd be more tasteful.'

Tiggy smiled. 'It took guts to wear it,' she said, cheering up.

'Yes, gutsy. We should sign her up to tackle Alicia!' Georgina joked.

The two women spontaneously burst out laughing, 'a huge hat, and a drunk fighting huge feet and a scary temper. 'Who'd win, I wonder?'

'Alicia!' they said emphatically together whilst giggling at the thought of the duel.

'Speaking of hats, did you see that young man hanging about outside the church?' Georgina asked.

Tiggy nodded. 'With the bucket hat and red holdall? He keeps popping up all over the place. He was even camped out with his bag near the Lightning Tree.'

'That's a bit odd!' Georgina replied, her eyes narrowing.

'He stopped by the track last night, but because of this,' Tiggy said, holding up Alicia's letter, 'it was all I could think about.'

'Any idea who he is, or what he's doing here?' Georgina enquired, looking slightly worried.

Tiggy shrugged, 'P'raps he's a scout or a spy from another club and it's a camera in the bag, after our training drills, sizing up the competition. I know he was checking us out.'

'You don't think he's stalking you, do you?'

'Don't be silly, Mum! I'm just not stalker material!'

'Don't be silly, sweetheart; there's no such thing. It can be anyone. I'm deadly serious!' Georgina retorted, seeing Tiggy grinning. 'He could have anything in that bag, and when I say 'anything' I mean ANYTHING!' Her eyes flashed danger. 'The sooner you get another housemate, the better!' she concluded, wafting the flyer again at her daughter and leaving it on the table.

❉❉❉❉❉❉❉❉❉❉❉❉

The next morning, the Heavenly Gardens residents and Alicia's newest recruits were on a mission and had gathered on the close. Dreary Greygoyles still dominated the place, although Father Time's grey hair and wrinkles, now arguably, made their dour and dowdy attitudes a tad more understandable. They judged and complained, strangling life and at their advancing years, had still not grasped that there are no second chances. Time had done nothing to change them or their prejudices. These were Alicia's people, stuck up, and stuck in Great Snubington. The Tipples' former home, 6, 'Pearly Gates', was now 'The Fountains' on account of a giant cascading Triton on the front lawn and a mermaid on the back. The owners, Mr and Mrs Harrington and their grown-up daughter Keira, were a hit with Alicia. Arthur Ramsbottom, still living next door, with the same twinkle in his eyes, said they seemed fine, but Tiggy was not so sure; anyone friends with Alicia automatically had a huge red flag. Noteworthy changes included, the Potters' grand, doorstep ornamental lions outstaying the couple who had moved into sheltered housing; the Gibsons having divorced and disappeared, whilst the Riches' stay was short and snappy, realising that they would never feel at home, and morbid James Cartwright had eventually passed on, having looked forward to his funeral for years. The Gotobeds were still around but keeping their distance. Their years of ugly spats with Alicia had not ended well, and the couple needed therapy and to withdraw to the far side of the village. Hugo F.

Uppingham was an even busier busybody these days, whilst the inoffensive, bird-loving Luvvies remained compliant and seldom seen, having swapped their noisy parrot for a budgerigar to keep the peace. The bird had headed Alicia's Banish List after a tirade of abusive language every time she passed Number 9.

The Greygoyles filed into the Grimshaws', the usual meeting place ever since Gertie had become wheelchair dependent. Alicia rattled her charm bracelet, sitting down next to a cabinet of gnomes. Gertie's vast collection had swallowed up the entire garden and had spread indoors.

'Are these new?' Alicia enquired, pointing at the cabinet as if she were interested. She wasn't.

Timothy Grimshaw glanced out of the living room window. Harry 'Flash' Dobson's new housekeeper, Beryl, was polishing the door knocker giving the brass a few extra rubs before discarding her cloth to join Ernest McAvey and Terence Tiddy, still known as the 'Ish Man,' because of how he spoke, and who were holding hands on their way to the meeting.

Alicia was pacing, eager to introduce Rach, the group's newest face.

'A little bird has told me, it's Rach's birthday; 21 again?' Alicia quipped, handing her a card.

'Aw, thanks, A,' Rach said, taking the card out of the envelope. Gary Barlow, one of her 'Take That' heartthrobs, was on the front. Rach fake swooned like a love-struck teenager. 'Such a dish!' she said, patting her chest.

'That's absolutely fantastic!' said a voice in a strong Mancunian accent, as she opened the talking card. It was unmistakably Gary's voice.

Rach giggled, 'Such a dish! I'll add it to my collection.'

The residents looked perplexed by the boy band super fan, old enough to be over it, a talking birthday card, and Alicia being nice. Rach didn't fit with Alicia's usual recruitment type, and they wondered whether there was more to Rach than met the eye. The super fan kissed Gary on the front of her card, unable to resist opening it again.

'That's absolutely fantastic,' Gary repeated.

'Can we get on with it?' Gertie Grimshaw snapped. 'You said it would be brief!'

She stared pointedly at Hugo as if it was his fault. Her wheelchair situation had made her even more like a bad-tempered wasp.

'Would anyone like some shortbread?' Ernest McAvey asked, trying to ease the tension.

Known for years as the 'shortbread man', he still took a tin to every meeting.

Hugo Uppingham cleared his throat before announcing the agenda for this impromptu Extraordinary

General Meeting. Beryl, already bored, ran her finger over a nearby ledge, checking for dust. Gertie Grimshaw's sharp and critical eyes saw it, her cheeks turning crimson, but her husband, Timothy, gallantly responded.

'Rude!' he said, stroking his head, his 'go to' self-comforting habit after parting with his wig. Gertie simmered down.

'Soz! It's just habit from working at H's and shining already shiny surfaces,' Beryl apologised, only to gaff again. 'You certainly wouldn't be safe at Number 2 with that shiny, bald head,' she said, staring at Timothy. 'I'd definitely give that a rub and a polish!'

Beryl looked across at Rach, instinctively knowing that they were two of a kind, and as their eyes locked, they burst out laughing, and seeing the stony faces in the room, they laughed even more. Nobody else did. Alicia was squirming, knowing that the 'newbies' were dropping clangers, but she needed numbers for her protest.

'Can we please get started?' Gertie asked, sounding irritated, and spinning around in her wheelchair to 'accidentally on purpose' run over Beryl's toes.

The first item drew a blank from the room when Glen Harrington enquired about a young man of distinctive looks and character, wearing a bucket hat, who had been loitering outside number 6 recently.

'I saw him looking at Keira's car in our driveway and making a note of her jewellery advert, and I wondered if he wanted her number to ask her out.'

'I've seen him. He's a hunk!' Rach said, critically looking the pretty, young woman up and down.

Hugo Uppingham concluded that the stranger was 'a person of interest' to keep an eye on. Moving on to the main reason for the crisis talks, Hugo read out Alicia's strategy for the ultimate closure of BMX Mania and Every Child Matters.

'But do we know that the kids are actually a threat to anything or anyone?' asked Beryl.

Alicia shook her head in disbelief, 'Of course they are! There's that kid I call 'Simple Simon' always prowling around, running on about how chainsaws work and the grisly things they can do.' Alicia's tone was emphatic.

'Yes, but...' Beryl retorted, expecting more.

'No yes but!' Alicia interrupted, 'Surely a maniac with a chainsaw should be enough!'

She was fuming and starting to pace the room. Everyone looked scared, and not of Simon and his hypothetical chainsaw.

'More shortbread?' Ernest asked, offering the tin around, hoping to calm things down. There was no chance.

'He recites his father's chainsaw manual, word for word, off by heart. What normal kid does that?' Alicia ranted.

'But might we be accused of being NIMBYs?' Timothy Grimshaw asked.

Beryl looked puzzled, 'NIMBYs?'

'Allow me to explain, my dear; it stands for 'not in my backyard'. In other words, it would be OK anywhere else but just not here, if that makes sense?' He sounded patronising.

'Gotcha!' Beryl said, staring at Alicia's 'rock', her famed massive diamond ring.

Ernest McAvey raised his hand to speak. 'Maybe we're judging them a wee bit prematurely?'

'Um, too soonish?' the 'Ish Man' agreed.

'I concur,' Timothy Grimshaw said. 'We've been protesting without really knowing about who or what.'

Alicia scowled at him, but everyone else started to question her, too.

'To be honest,' Gertie Grimshaw said, cradling Bertie, her newest gnome, 'I felt a bit guilty after we caused all that commotion at the wedding. Daisy Dingles pushed me in my chair and gave me some of her confetti.'

'Bonnie lass!' said Ernest. 'Could it be, Alicia, that you have more of an issue with the Tipples than the children themselves?'

Timothy nodded, 'You always had it in for them when they left the Close.'

Alicia audibly scoffed, 'Ridiculous!'

'Just tell them something bad that these children have done,' Rach suggested, trying to help her.

'Um...' Alicia mumbled, gazing into space, trying desperately to think of something.

'One wee lassie has the voice of an angel; her singing brings me to tears,' Ernest said.

'Divinish!' Terence agreed.

'And Omara is an incredible dancer,' Glen Harrington joined in, 'I, personally, made him all his dance shoes to improve his in-step.'

His wife smiled, 'Penelope has uncovered a real talent there.'

Hugo Uppingham nodded. 'Not forgetting that Tiggy, love her or hate her, is training those kids to be winners and track stars like her,' he said with a surprising change of attitude.

Alicia was seething. Had Hugo, her second in command as she saw him, just turned on her?

'What is this?' Alicia asked in dismay.

'They're certainly putting Great Snubington on the map for something positive after so many years of the curse and awful news headlines. It was all this place was known for.' Hugo was speaking in everyone's defence.

'What about Simple Simon?' Alicia scowled, 'I've already told you about his chainsaw obsession. He regurgitates the manual word for word.'

'That's proper smart, though,' Beryl said, staring at Alicia's ring again.

Timothy Grimshaw looked impressed. 'He must have a photographic memory.'

'Smart?' Alicia exclaimed. Her indignation was obvious. 'What is this? 'A disagree with Alicia' meeting? It's a witch hunt!' she screamed.

'It's no such thing, my dear Alicia. I just think that we might be over-reacting slightly,' Hugo said, trying to calm Alicia's mood. 'Just because Simon knows about chainsaws doesn't mean anything. He's always working his Rubik's cube whenever I've seen him.'

'It's a disaster waiting to happen.' Alicia's barbed tone met with mumbled disagreement.

'But they're just children,' Keira whispered to her parents. 'Surely they deserve a chance?'

Alicia blundered on, 'So are we all agreed on my plans?' Her steely stare penetrated the room, and the atmosphere was so uncomfortable that Rach opened her birthday card again.

'That's absolutely fantastic!' This time Gary's voice made everyone laugh, except for Alicia.

'Are we agreed?' Alicia persisted, increasingly annoyed by the dissenting whispers:

'Harmless youngsters,' 'sweet, wee things,' 'talented kids,' were ringing in her ears.

Glen Harrington nudged his wife Glenda, who in turn nudged their daughter, looking visibly upset.

'It's plain mean! Kids bullied by adults!' Keira complained.

"Mean?" I'm always buying your jewellery, your mother's hats, and your father's shoes. I must have kept all three of your businesses afloat this past year, and you have the cheek to call me 'mean!' Talk about gratitude!'

It was partly true. Alicia had been their best customer and was the reason for their being there. The room fell silent again, and Terence Tiddy was jittering, knowing how brutal Alicia had been with the Gotobeds: her vendetta had been relentless until she had broken them and driven them off the estate as nervous wrecks.

'Perhaps not 'mean' but 'meanish,' Terence said, emboldened by Ernest's hand on his leg, stopping his jittering knee.

Alicia glared at them both.

'And I thought you were my friends! It's like this,' Alicia said, circling the room, stopping by every individual to stare menacingly into their eyes. 'I've got dirty little secrets on you all...' she threatened, 'and I'm certainly ready and happy to spill.'

Alicia swung her head to look Hugo Uppingham directly in the eyes. The man, who was usually a model of composure, looked shocked and visibly rattled. Alicia knew far too much about his dishonest and dodgy tax returns for him not to take her threat seriously. Fortunately, he knew how to schmooze.

'You are, of course, right, my dear, wise Alicia. We all know that people have said that 'bad things happen when good people do nothing.' Hugo was in full diplomatic, damage limitation mode and stared with intensity at all the worried faces to bring them on side.

'And we are good people,' Gertie responded from her wheelchair. Her husband nodded, triggering a wave of nods around the room. Everyone knew that Alicia was ruthless and prepared to play dirty.

'All those in favour of Alicia's proposals to close BMX Mania and Every Child Matters,' Hugo asked, and seeing a clean sweep of hands, he declared the motion carried unanimously.

Alicia grinned and, grabbing Rach's card off her lap, she opened it, allowing Gary Barlow to have the final, 'That's absolutely fantastic!' to celebrate.

Chapter 7

THE '-BER' MONTHS

We are but a grain in the sands of time. Nearly a year had passed since Tiggy had lost her father the day before her 29th birthday. The tragedy automatically steamrollered the usual celebrations, and it was as if turning 29 had never actually happened, and from that moment, any future birthdays would be unavoidably scarred and never quite the same again. Her 30th birthday certainly didn't feel like a cause for celebration, but Georgina Tipple was determined to put on a brave face along with her favourite mascara and lipstick to make something of it, just as Thomas would have wanted. A small surprise gathering of family and friends lay in wait at Arthur Ramsbottom's place, a plan he had hatched with Georgina, having invited Tiggy to drop in for 'birthday cake and bubbles but nothing fancy.'

It had been a beautiful day of gentle warmth on bare shoulders, but Tiggy did not feel it inside. Life was cold since the chapter closed on that part of family life, when jobs had either 'been jobbed' or were 'about to be jobbed'. The loss of her father and, more recently, of Gav had widened the yawning abyss left by dear Mrs D's passing. There had been a plot twist in her story, with important characters now missing who should have fleshed out more chapters. On the poignant eve of her 30th birthday, her life story didn't seem such a 'good read' anymore, given the close succession of shattering events.

It was just after 7 o'clock, and the Lightning Tree, bathed in a golden light, cast its magic upon the glowing earth, set afire by the sinking sun falling like a swollen blood orange towards the pink horizon. It was as if Salvador Dali had visited with his paintbox, leaving behind a surreal dreamscape for the universe. Over recent months, Tiggy had buried herself in her business, training her students at her biking academy. She stayed busy out of choice to keep the darkness at bay because alone, delving deeper into her thoughts, she was a prisoner awaiting freedom to find the bright light of happiness again. Tiggy stared at the tree, its clawed, contorted branches pointing up into the evening sky; it was her new constant, her every day, from sunrise to sunset, always there waiting. They had history in common, both so savagely wounded by an unexpected event, testing their strength and resilience, and yet they stayed standing.

'I'm like you now,' Tiggy mumbled to the tree's ghostly branches, 'but like you, I will rise again.'

Tiggy cycled on until she reached the perfectly mowed lawns of Heavenly Gardens, just in time to see Beryl clocking off for the day, having given Harry 'Flash' Dobson his evening meal and settling him in for the night. Past birthdays were flooding her head, and yet she always came back to the same, life-affirming memory—her unforgettable 10th birthday when her father wheeled in a sparkling, new stunt cycle at her first-ever party. After her rainbow adventures twenty years earlier, her world had changed for the better until now. Mrs D had told her that 'good things come to those who wait', so despite her world feeling cold and dark, she just needed to be patient and trust in time taking her to a warmer, brighter place.

Tiggy walked into Arthur's living room, and a huddle of family faces and a few parents and riders from the academy burst into 'Happy Birthday'. A film show was playing in the background on a large screen of Tiggy from birth to thirty.

'Not the baby photos, please!' Tiggy moaned playfully.

'Just thought your young riders should see you in action,' Arthur commented. 'It's not every village that has its own world champion.'

Tiggy smiled. 'If I can inspire just one of them to follow in my tyre tracks, it might not be so bad turning 30 after all!' she said, looking at her youngsters watching in awe at her racing and winning.

'I knew you were good, Miss, but not that good,' Mikey Junior said, glued to the screen, 'your corners are mental!'

'What a legend!' Michaela declared.

'The Girls' stared at her and whispered, giggling between themselves. Michaela didn't care; she was a twin, and that gave her steel.

The gathering was a surprise, but with slices of cake and bubbles at the movies, the occasion Tiggy had dreaded for days had turned into a far better birthday than ever she could have hoped.

Life moved on, and with the '-ber' months already upon them, the young man with the red holdall, still regarded as a strange face in the village, and a 'person of interest' to watch, continued to cause a bit of a stir. Nobody knew much about him, and the villagers didn't like it. He would usually appear in the village store to make a random purchase, often of peanut butter, and then disappear for a bit until he popped up again, presumably when he had run out of the spread. However, on his last visit he had asked to buy 'winter squash' and had bought the largest pumpkin in the store. Timothy Grimshaw, who was there buying a loaf of bread, made a note to report this sighting at the resident's next meeting.

Tiggy loved this time of year. The leaves had turned to amber and gold, carpeting the ground for feet to crunch, and although the dappled sun was weak, it was softer and still shining, as autumn asserted itself and smiled farewell to summer. However, without leaves to shed, the Lightning Tree still looked the same. Whatever the season, the tree embraced the change, a steadfast spirit that Tiggy admired, and rewarded each Halloween by carving a giant pumpkin to sit at its base. It became her 'Ghost Tree' and a spooky reminder of the storm's curse that had befallen the village all those years before.

This Halloween, many of the village children were doing the rounds, 'Trick or Treating'. MJ was dressed as a vampire, his mouth running with fake blood, Micky, a cute black cat, had drawn-on whiskers, pointy ears, and a fabulous swishy tail, whilst Scotty and Robbo were hiding beneath white bed sheets, making spooky noises as ghosts. It was dusk, and they were hoping to be the first 'Trick or Treaters' to call.

'We need to go to the posh homes first,' Robbo said, leading the way to Heavenly Gardens, 'and beat anyone else to the best stuff, 'cos once it's gone, it's gone!'

'We want cash!' Scotty said in a muffled voice because of the sheet. 'That Gold woman is minted; let's try her first.'

It was a brave child who would knock on Alicia Gold's door, but MJ did. He was as fearless doing this as he was at slick manoeuvres on the track. The others, hiding around the corner of the house, were spying, ready to jump out when the door opened. At first, nobody came, and so MJ knocked a bit harder. A curtain twitched upstairs, and then the window opened.

'Trick or Treat?' MJ shouted, looking up at the window.

'Trick,' Alicia yelled back as she tipped a bucket of water on top of him. Alicia cackled as MJ left, soaked from head to toe, looking like a scalded cat.

'I'm going straight home!' MJ said, overturning Alicia's wheelie-bin and spreading the rubbish across the drive. Micky looked horrified.

'She did say 'Trick!' Robbo mumbled with guilty justification as they fled the Close.

A few of the girls from ECM and their mothers were also doing the rounds of the village. Sophie, Grace and Blessings, dressed as witches and carrying fake cauldrons and broomsticks, knocked at the homes with a pumpkin on the doorstep. The girls were nervous, but a few houses in, their cauldrons were brimming with goodies. As a thank you, the girls twirled around in their costumes, pretending to cast a 'good luck' spell. They were just leaving Nightingale Road when they passed the wet and bedraggled vampire, MJ, and friends.

'We should have dressed as witches!' Micky said, envying the girls' full cauldrons.

'Nah! We just shouldn't have visited one!' Scotty quipped, making everyone laugh.

They passed 'The Lads' and 'The Girls', jostling them in jest, eventually catching up with Bo and her mother, Rach, who were wandering the streets dressed in clingy, bright red devil costumes and carrying a pumpkin lantern.

'I hope we see the fit stranger guy,' Rach said, adjusting her horns and wiggling her devil's tail. 'I'd love to knock on his door and ask him for a treat!'

Rach and Bo's paths didn't cross with Todd that night, but somebody else's very nearly did:

Tiggy had arrived at the Lightning Tree, her 'Ghost Tree' for the night. The air was crisp and nippy, the moon and stars lighting the tree's knobbly branches to creepy effect. Her Ghost Tree was like an imaginary bridge, connecting the physical world with something more, something spiritual beyond even the stars. This was the one night of the year when in the darkness, Tiggy felt an inner light, as if her Ghost Tree had surrendered its powers to her, an anchor, and support regardless of whatever life's whirlwinds and tempests were in her midst. She felt invincible, and in gratitude, she placed her carved-out pumpkin beneath the tree, its flame flickering brightly, casting a yellow light upon the ground. Here she would leave the flame to dance until it burnt itself out. However, this Halloween she was amazed to find an enormous pumpkin, beautifully carved, already burning beneath the tree. Someone else, someone unknown, had beaten her to her Ghost Tree. It was Todd. He had left the pumpkin mere minutes before she arrived.

By bonfire night, the pumpkins were starting to turn a bit squishy. MJ and his biker friends, having failed dismally on Halloween to get any money, were now on a mission to make up for it. Scotty was full of ideas and had soon rustled up a dummy from an old pillow, clothes and scrunched up newspaper, for them to cart around the village in Robbo's dad's wheelbarrow, asking for 'a Penny for the Guy'. Timothy Grimshaw, pushing his wife in her wheelchair, stopped to feel for loose change in his pockets.

'Keep going!' Gertie ordered. 'They're just begging again. On Halloween it was for 'treats' when what they really wanted was money, and now it's to celebrate burning a Catholic!' she moaned, crossing herself and clutching her rosary beads. Gertie glared at the children, shaking her head. 'I blame the parents,' she griped in such a scathing voice that it scared the children enough to push the wheelbarrow as quickly as they could to find 'some nice people' somewhere else.

They had already collected a few coins outside the village store when Arthur Ramsbottom gave them a £5 note. He remembered how much he had loved collecting the burnt firework shells as a boy. This time of year, the memories always came flooding back, of his last walk with his twin and their dog on the ill-fated night of the storm. They had been hunting for firework shells at the time, so in that moment of the children asking for firework money, he would gladly have emptied his pockets, wallet, and bank account to take one more walk with his brother Arnold again.

Arthur hobbled with his stick into the shop, politely nodding to Alicia Gold, who was on her way out.

'Look! It's the witch!' Micky whispered behind her hand.

Alicia stared at the group who had frozen to the spot, lost for words, and smirked at the home-made figure slumped inside the wheelbarrow, as she noticed the sign.

'Penny for the Guy,' she read aloud. To the children's amazement, Alicia took out her purse.

Scotty nudged Robbo, who in turn nudged MJ.

'I reckon it's an apology,' whispered Robbo, watching Alicia sifting through her purse and clutching several pound coins in her left hand.

The children's eyes flashed at each other with excitement, hoping for a generous donation. However, this was Alicia Gold. She separated the nickel brass coins from the coppers, dropping a one pence coin into the Guy's hat so that everyone could see.

'Well, you asked for a penny, so you've got one!' she said, looking at the shocked and disappointed faces, and laughing like a braying donkey, she walked away.

A few days later, it was Arthur Ramsbottom's 80th birthday. He didn't want any fuss but invited Tiggy and her family to a picnic by the Lightning Tree.

'It's Arnold's 80th, too, so I thought the place we spent our last moments together would be fitting,' he said and so, they all wrapped up well and had a picnic by the tree: a simple spread for a simple man wishing to remember his brother, just a boy of simple pleasures.

Winter was approaching, and an icy wind was blowing away the first full year without Thomas Tipple. The months had disappeared so fast as the family faced the many challenges and first times of doing life's occasions and traditions, carving out their new normal. Last Christmas Thomas's passing was fresh and raw, and there was no tree, their woodland spruce having stayed firmly in the ground. However, this year, Adam was on 'digging duty' to uproot the specially selected spruce previously marked with the 'X', by Thomas Tipple.

The cold snap had brought with it an early flurry of snow and as Tiggy, Penelope, and Adam headed with a spade towards the woods on the Tipple's farmland, their Wellington boots left tracks as far as the chosen tree. The evergreen, still fully clad, seemed to defy the cold whilst other trees shivered in the bitter wind, their naked branches stripped bare and dressed in snow. Tiggy stared at the silhouetted beauty of the bare trees, thinking how they now looked like the Lightning Tree on any day of the year.

As December progressed, the stranger with the campervan and red holdall was noticeable by his absence. The residents of Heavenly Gardens surmised that he was gone for good, but they were wrong. Thanksgiving had beckoned Todd back to his homeland, and having feasted with family on turkey and stocked up on love, he was back to continue where he had left off. Todd had decked out his campervan with tinsel, and he was wearing a new thick, plush winter's coat and a fur deerstalker hat. There was a single sighting of him near the church, and then he disappeared again.

The Advent calendar at Every Child Matters had most of its doors open when a courier arrived with a special delivery of 'impossible to find' purple wrapping paper. Daisy Dingles had written to Santa asking for 'a purple present' with no further explanation or details offered. Therefore, with Daisy's expectations focussed on purple, there would be no triggering surprises, and the present would be purple, both the contents and paper. Leeroy, who liked what he knew, had chosen the gift he wanted from Mr Claus, and was happy to watch as his mother wrapped it. He didn't wish to meet Mr Claus under any circumstances, no matter how kind he was. The festive season brought its challenges to Every Child Matters but also to Penelope, who was learning all the time to adapt the activities to what the children needed rather than what she hoped they wanted. In fact, it had caused a minor tiff between the otherwise happy newlyweds.

'You're not thinking of Theo or the others like him, you're thinking of yourself!' Adam criticised Penelope for proposing a traditional Christmas party with Christmas songs and games as an ECM first.

'I just want them to be excited and have fun,' Penelope said, managing her disappointment.

Adam shook his head, 'I thought we were past all that, and you understood. Fun is different things to different people.'

There would be no 'Secret Santa', flashing lights or loudly played Christmas songs to bombard their senses, and Mr Claus would stay away, just leaving their gifts by the tree on the morning of 23rd December, after 22 more sleeps. However, instead, there would be a silent disco, allowing the guests control over their own individual play list and volume.

In contrast, at BMX Mania, the festive songs were blasting out from the old windmill at their Christmas bash. 'The Girls' surprised everyone, arriving in matching tops emblazoned with 'I'm on Santa's Naughty List'. Mikey Junior was wearing an elf hat and ears, whilst Scotty, as usual, outdid the lot with a fake turkey stuck on his head that had everyone laughing and wanting to try it on. After months of hard training in all weathers, it was time to have some fun. Robbo's Secret Santa fake dog poop tricked a few people, whilst Tiggy opened her mystery gift of a 'Grow Your Own Boyfriend' with good humour. The kids were right; the tiny rubber figure, once soaked in water, would be a less troublesome pocket-sized 'other half' than hers in real life.

The Christmas tree was the focal point of the festivities in Tiggy's farmhouse home. The fairy lights twinkled and the angel hair shimmered, softening and blurring the branches and melting the bright colours into a muted, dreamy haze. Each day the presents were building beneath the tree, Buddy sniffing the pile for any that were his.

It was Christmas Eve morning and carols were playing in the background whilst Penelope and Tiggy, fuelled by mulled wine and mince pies, were prepping the food for the following day, vying to go to the top of Santa's 'good list.'

However, somebody else's name was already at the top of that list.

A white van pulled up outside, followed by footsteps. Buddy and also Penelope's greyhound Nureyev ran to the door.

'Special delivery for Every Child Matters,' the couriers said, standing a massive, slatted container on the doorstep. Something was moving inside it, and hay was poking through the open slats. It was Alex's gift to them all: two baby miniature donkeys to join the other therapy animals.

Whilst Christmas Day was soon in full swing at the farmhouse, elsewhere, Todd was celebrating amongst strangers at a soup kitchen in the nearest city. Christmas is so many things to different people, often with family at its heart, but to Todd, alone and many miles from home, he was giving a piece of his to others.

THE EX

A blanket of snow had fallen, covering the earth with the purest of light. The Lightning Tree was always the weather's witness. In the chilly breeze, the gnarled branches shivered, reaching up like the hands of Old Man Winter, catching the falling flakes and adding soft accents to the silvery wood. It was a new year and a time of reflection and resolutions. A few months had passed since Tiggy's heart-to-heart chat with her mother about life beyond the track, and as Tiggy looked in the mirror, she could see the truth staring back at her. It wasn't what was there, but that her glow and sparkle wasn't. The light had gone out in her eyes, and she hadn't been honest with her mother. The bottom line was that she wasn't completely over her ex. Gav wanted her back and had persuaded her (she suspected, too easily) to meet up to talk things through. Gav was predictable: he would claim to have changed just as he had done so many times before. It had meant nothing. Gav talked 'a good story'.

There were three benches on the village playing field: the 'Knit More Nora' unveiled twenty years earlier by Penelope, the then Fun Day princess, and another of sturdy oak bearing a large shiny plaque in memory of the village's 14 curse victims. Call it bad karma or superstition, many of the villagers refused to sit on it, but today, surprisingly, the young man with the bucket hat (swapped out for his furry deerstalker) and red holdall was there watching the world go by despite the bitter, biting cold. However, on the third and most recent bench sited by the rustic pavilion, Gav was waiting. This bench was special to Tiggy, and if anything could fix their broken relationship, it would happen here. Hand-carved from a fallen oak once standing in Mrs Derbyshire's wood, the bench was the place she thought stuff through, and got her messy head right, re-igniting the world champion mindset from a low point in her life. When her father passed, Alicia had started and spread a vicious rumour that the curse had struck again, but the village, having lived curse-free for nineteen years, had not given Alicia or her rumour, oxygen. Tiggy often brought Buddy here to daydream and to remember the times when, in her father's words, jobs were 'jobbed'.

Tiggy had not seen Gav in many months, and seeing her ex in his winter warmers and the scarf she had bought him, sitting on her special bench, she fought the smile creeping onto her lips.

'Hey!' Gav said with a huge grin as they fist bumped, 'I've missed your little face!'

Tiggy lost her battle not to smile. It was annoying, just like Gav. She was going to be frosty, but Tiggy could feel the ice around her heart already beginning to melt. Gav grinned and nodded as though he knew he was about to reel her in, but if anything like Tiggy of old, she would put up a fight. Gav stared into her shining green eyes,

'So have you missed me?' he asked, keeping eye contact.

'Nah!' Tiggy replied, determined not to be a pushover. If the flames were to re-ignite, Gav would have to graft.

'Not even a little bit?'

Tiggy hesitated.

'You have! I knew it!' Gav grinned. His cheeky charm and chat had always worked with the girls. Gav thought of it as his 'superpower'. The ice had thawed a tiny bit more, and deep down, Tiggy thought that a part of her wanted it to.

'You're looking good, Tiggywig,' Gav said. Only he called her that, and it was giving her a warm, squidgy feeling inside. She knew that after 6 months of them being over, it shouldn't. Tiggy's head was spinning; never had she felt so conflicted. Gav had been the only one for whom she had ever dropped the 'L' bomb, and he had, too, but maybe she hadn't known what love was, and she should never have said it. She wondered if love and being in love were different things to different people.

It felt like a mess, but Gav was using his killer smile, looking deep into her eyes, penetrating the ice around her heart, chatting about the good times. Tiggy could feel the thaw and her tough exterior turning to goo as Gav continued to rekindle their best bits and happy memories. Gav knew how to play a girl.

The voices in Tiggy's head had started. 'What are you doing? Are you letting him in again?'

Tiggy knew she was, but was determined that her walls should stay up for now.

'So, are you still hanging out with Jack?' Tiggy asked, already aware of the answer. She had heard enough to know that the two lads were still out every weekend in the bars and clubs collecting hearts. A little ice reformed.

'Not much,' Gav lied, conscious of how much Tiggy disliked his mate.

'Do you remember the first time we came here, and I'd bought you a sausage roll?' Gav asked, trying to deflect from Jack and any further tricky questions. 'You hadn't told me you're a veggie and you just picked off the pastry saying how 'yum' it was! I often chuckle about that.'

Tiggy smiled, remembering how much she had wanted to like the sausage roll to please him. Tiggy wasn't typically a 'people pleaser', but in that moment she had been.

'So, have you been seeing anyone?' Tiggy asked, realising she shouldn't care unless she was still interested in patching things up with him.

Gav paused and looked sheepish, 'Not really.'

'I'll take that as a 'yes' then,' Tiggy's response was ice cold. She gazed away to collect her thoughts, noticing the mystery stranger in the deerstalker hat sitting on the curse memorial bench staring at them.

'Who's he?' Gav enquired, happy to change the subject.

'Dunno. I've seen him about.'

'He's a decent-looking guy, but a bit of a creep! He can't keep his eyes off you, I reckon he fancies you.'

'If you say so,' Tiggy replied, disconnected from the current conversation and still thinking about Gav's answer. She glanced across to the bench as the man unzipped his red holdall and peered inside. Suddenly a female voice startled her from behind. She was young, barely out of school, with smudged heavy eyeliner and wearing a candy pink puffer jacket. Gav looked ashen.

'I knew it!' the young girl shouted, looking angry, her cheeks flushed, and a blotchy red rash appearing on her neck. 'I'm over her,' you said; 'she's a psycho,' you said; 'it's you, I love,' you said.' She started to cry. Gav gulped.

'It's not how it looks, Lils,' Gav responded.

'Still just the same ol' Gav!' Tiggy said with disdain. 'I'm nobody's option and she shouldn't be either!' and she walked away without a second glance.

Somebody had watched it all, and that somebody, the good-looking man on the curse's bench, picked up his holdall and began to follow her.

✿ ✿ ✿ ✿ ✿ ✿ ✿ ✿ ✿ ✿ ✿ ✿

The Gav chapter was complete, and Tiggy felt lighter for it. The sight of the young girl crying and the raw emotion was powerful: it was like looking at herself in the mirror. She would be moving on.

It was a spontaneous decision of Tiggy's to attend the February speed house-mating event; she had nothing to lose, and a housemate to gain. She scanned the room of tables full of wannabe tenants. Would anyone accept her habits?: her love and overuse of marmite, dirty socks in random places, walking and talking weird stuff in her sleep, things in odd places, such as keys in the dirty laundry or a thirsty house plant to be sharing the bath.

There were some dubious characters amongst the mix, including the blast from her past, 'Mikey Mucus,' the father of her star BMX students, MJ and Micky, as they were known at the track.

'What brings you here?' Tiggy asked, thinking how time had not been kind to Mikey since they were kids together. These days, he looked burdened and almost middle-aged, like many of the other 'cool kids' at school.

'The ex wants me out to move her new fella in,' Mikey said, biting his nails.

The cheeky chappy who Tiggy had always known, had disappeared.

'What about the twins? Will they stay with Sapph?'

Mikey shook his head, 'Not now she's got the sprog.'

'Awh! It makes me so sad when high school sweethearts break up,' Tiggy said, remembering how Mikey, the cheeky, cool maverick, and Sapphire, the gorgeous, 'hot' girl who all the boys fancied, had been such a 'power couple' at school.

'We were just kids having kids, so it was never likely to work out,' Mikey said with a maturity that surprised her. Tiggy nodded, pondering over the predicament.

'I don't think there's room for both you and the twins,' Tiggy said, feeling awkward at her lame excuse.

'I get it. They're a handful,' Mikey said, marking an 'x' in the box for Tiggy's table number.

She felt guilty not seeing it as a match.

Next up was a female calling herself 'Cat Woman'. She had five cats that would require a 'cat flap' fitted before moving in. Tiggy was sure she heard her meow on leaving her table for the next one. A man with a nut allergy followed, and a young woman with such long and fancy nails that Tiggy suspected they would rule her out of any household chores. Next up was a bookworm with a mountain of paperbacks to house and a middle-aged carer who reeked of alcohol, sneaking a tipple from a hip flask between tables. Another man had decent chat and an easy manner, but he came with a set of drums and a trumpet. Tiggy was running out of options for a match, and then, a late arrival changed everything: it was the stranger in the deerstalker hat. He was only interested in Tiggy's table. He sat down with purpose and a big smile, plonking his red holdall down on the floor. He took off his hat, shook her hand, introducing himself as 'Todd'. Tiggy looked at his shaved head and his trendy clothes.

'Nice jacket!' Tiggy said, thinking he was a cool cat and a promising housemate. 'I've seen you around a bit lately.'

'Yeah, I've been about when I'm not at my 9 to 5 in the city. It's a slog but it pays.'

'And spare time?' Tiggy enquired.

'Gotta campervan I hang loose in, but baseball is my big thing.'

'So, how d'ya do that around here?' Tiggy asked, intrigued by his accent.

'I wanna bring it to you Brits and start a league,' Todd said. 'Getting the kids involved. There's no reason they can't play soccer and baseball.'

'Are there any clubs here?'

'Not many, Miss!'

'It's Tiggy!'

'Cool name!...Tiggy!' he repeated with a grin as if he were hearing it for the first time.

'You're not from these parts?' she asked to confirm the accent that sounded like diluted American.

'I am now, but I'm from the States.'

'And,' Tiggy probed, staring into his popping blue eyes, 'why would you choose Great Snubington?'

'I guess I've been searching for something or someone...'

'And have you ...found it?'

'Maybe,' he said with a grin.

'Intriguing!' she said, holding the eye contact. Have you found anywhere for your baseball?'

Todd shook his head. 'I'm looking; it may take me a while to find somewhere,' he said, gazing down at his red holdall.

Tiggy liked him. Todd would be a perfect housemate, and she wanted to make sure he would tick her box as a match.

'There's loads of land at my place, perfect for your club, if you move in!'

The bell rang for the next rotation. Todd didn't hang about, putting on his hat and leaving without handing in his matches at the desk.

'Perhaps we weren't the match I thought we were,' Tiggy mumbled under her breath, seeing him leave and secretly feeling gutted that the offer of the land hadn't sealed the deal. At least if she saw him around 'Snubs' again, she would know he wasn't the stalker with a weapon in his bag that her mother had painted.

'Plenty more fish!' she mumbled.

Chapter 9

THE NEW HOUSEMATE

It was just over a week later that an old Volkswagen campervan pulled up outside Tiggy's farmhouse. It was Todd. He had returned later with his housemate match after Tiggy had left. She had been wrong to doubt him: they had both known instantly they were a fit, and now Todd was moving in.

'I'm not a stickler for rules,' Tiggy told Todd as he lugged his stuff inside. 'Leave things as you wish to find them, and on Fridays, we take turns to go into town and get the chippy tea. That's about it.'

They were Penelope's rules that Tiggy had often broken. Buddy, as usual, was chief 'meet and greeter' and was all over Todd, wagging his tail excitedly at having another special human to fuss over him.

'Buddy! Leave Todd and his things alone!' Tiggy ordered, as Buddy started sniffing at Todd's red holdall like a beagle with a bag full of drugs.

It was the same red holdall she had seen Todd with many times before, and that had made her mother suspicious. He moved the bag away from Buddy's nose, stroking his greying chin until the dog slumped down onto the bean bags. The new housemate travelled light, and apart from baseball bats, balls and helmets stowed in the back of the campervan, he had little else other than his clothes.

'Did you see any protesters on your way here?' Tiggy enquired. 'They're trying to shut us down.'

Todd removed his bucket hat and shook his shaven scalp.

'Makes a change!' she said, looking puzzled.

'Perhaps, they've given up?' Todd suggested, his eyes scanning his new home.

Tiggy shook her head, 'You don't know Alicia Gold, but you soon will. She's like a Rottweiler on steroids guarding a bone. There'll be no letting go. We're on her 'Banish List'.

'Sounds like starting a baseball club with her on the rampage might be awkward. Your Alicia…' he began picking up his holdall.

She isn't my Alicia, trust me!' Tiggy interjected. 'Even more reason to start one. Alicia loathes anything American!'

'That's me done then! She'll 100 per cent think I suck,' Todd said, turning his accent on full and grinning.

Her eyes moved to her new housemate's red holdall. Todd had it with him each time she had seen him. There was something intriguing about how he guarded and protected it, seldom putting it down, his eyes glued to it, constantly checking its whereabouts. In fact, she was right to be curious: there was nothing ordinary about the holdall and its contents.

'I'll leave you to unpack,' Tiggy said, showing Todd his room, and when she closed the door behind her, with Buddy at her side, she thought how happy her mother would be.

Todd sat down on the side of the bed and sighed. Tiggy didn't know who he really was. He had waited a long time, dreaming about meeting her again and imagining what this moment would be like. He couldn't tell her that he was that same boy she had met trapped in the rainbow all those years ago when they were 'the chosen ones', two Rainbow Children on a mission. He looked so different now. Todd, back then, was a skinny new teenager with bolted braces on his teeth, a riot of long dreadlocks and pimples. The young Tiggy knew him as the 'Stig Man'. Now he was Todd, a good-looking 'thirty something', tall and muscular with a shaved scalp, a dazzling smile that flashed his perfect teeth and small scars on his chin and forehead. He had certainly grown into his looks. Todd's release from the Indigo and its dark forces was at its best, dramatic, and at its worst, traumatic, but after many years in a wilderness trying to make sense of his journey and to be someone he wasn't, he was finally here with Tiggy again, the real Todd. Apart from his holdall, it felt like all that mattered. Todd fiddled with a lock, unzipped the bag, peeping inside, and smiling zipped it up again. It was a truth bound in secrecy and risk.

'I'll be gone for a bit,' Tiggy called from the kitchen on her way out.

Todd looked out of the window. He could see Tiggy slow biking with Buddy lolloping alongside her, doing his best to keep up. He watched them fade to a speck until they eventually disappeared. He glanced around at this simple place of bean bags, cushions, a comfy, plush sofa, and fireside rocking chairs, already feeling at home. His search was over, and he'd found what he had been looking for all these years.

In the kitchen, like any typical young male with a good appetite, he checked out the fridge, stocked with milk, butter, eggs, and a lonely garlic bulb. Some well-used garden clippers were on the windowsill; they had belonged to Tiggy's green-fingered father, and nobody had used them since he passed. The roses rambled freely these days. Todd's eyes flashed to the 'Mrs Always Right' and 'Mr Handsome' mugs on the draining board; maybe Tiggy had a special someone in her life that explained her leaving.

His tour continued into the living room, settling into one of the bleached wood fireside chairs, rocking back and forth. He felt at peace, relaxed, contented, at home. There wasn't that much to see: a Venetian mask, a cuckoo clock and a goldfish bowl full of various countries' flags. It was the same bowl that Alex had worn when pretending to be an astronaut. Todd knew none of this stuff, and as his eyes roved the room, they settled upon the mantelpiece. The elegant figurine that little Tiggy always moved from the hall table during the Heavenly Gardens' days, (knowing her mother would move it back again) was overseeing a crystal rock. It was the sparkling, speckled chunk of midnight blue lapis lazuli that he had given Tiggy before she had left him for the 'Indigo Realm' all those years ago. Seeing the rock sitting there between the figurine on one side, and a postcard of Wales and a box of tissues on the other, seemed so out of context and a million miles away from where it first came. He couldn't stop thinking about it, and as he rocked in his chair, his mind drifted back to the rainbow. He remembered the moment he first met the lively, fresh-faced Tiggy who was so lost and confused, and unaware of the journey ahead. He had taught her 'what's what' and the rainbow 'dos and don'ts.' It had been epic, each Rainbow Realm having an incredible story that even now still blew his mind. Those times he had cherished and locked away: they were his, but more importantly, they were also 'theirs'; they were his strength in troubled times, but an invisible anchor day to day when he was simply keeping on keeping on. Just like the four-leafed clover Tiggy had given him, the memories woven into his heart were a part of him. He wished that all of them were good, but some were the opposite and were playing out in his head once more. At the edge of the Indigo Realm, he had told Tiggy that his crystal would protect her, and it seemed like it had. Right now, seeing how she had kept it, his heart felt full, and he had no doubt that this was where he belonged.

Todd stepped outside and breathed in the cool, fresh February air. It was a desolate scene of frosty meadows and steely skies, and despite the addition of 'Every Child Matters' in a converted barn and the BMX track, it was a glorious slice of countryside. Alicia, of course, regarded them as 'a noisy, ugly blot on the landscape', putting them at the top of her 'Banish List'. The distant chant of her gang, protesting and doing what they did best, wafted in on the breeze. Todd didn't fully understand the village's internal squabbles, but he knew that they were spiteful, targeting Tiggy's family and a handful of children trying to find their place in the world. He suspected that he, too, would soon become part of Alicia's problem with his ambitious baseball plans to bring a fabulously unapologetic chunk of America to 'Little England'.

However, for now, his dreams and schemes were far from his thoughts; it was his red holdall bossing them.

Todd took hold of the gold zip, fiddled with the combination lock's dial clipped onto the zipper, and opened the large, red canvas bag, setting it down in the old herb garden, the prime spot for winter sun. Mrs Derbyshire had often joked that in summer the buff York stone slabs were hot enough to fry an egg on them. Todd wandered around to the back of the farmhouse where the old wooden barrel, the once fictitious home of the Boggle, was standing full of freshly fallen rain, and removing a water bottle from the outer pouch of the holdall, he filled it to the brim.

'We're gonna be fine, Seraphina, I promise,' Todd murmured, staring inside the bag. He squeezed the bottle, carefully pouring a few drops of rainwater into the holdall, unable to dislodge thoughts of how he came to be there:

When Tiggy had left the 'Stig Man' in the dark and sinister world of the Indigo, his story, now Todd's story, was incomplete. It seemed that only a miracle would save him. That miracle was Angel Seraphina, Tiggy's rainbow angel, who had sacrificed herself to help him.

Todd peeped into his holdall, feeling the sun beating down on the back of his neck, and smiled with gratitude at Angel Seraphina staring back at him, her eyes wide open.

✻✻✻✻✻✻✻✻✻✻✻✻

Tiggy, in fact, had gone to see her 'Significant Other' but just not in the romantic sense. She often visited Arthur Ramsbottom, who had always encouraged and watched her soar to her dreams. She described him, as 'class', and their bond was unbreakable. He was everything that most of the Heavenly Gardens' residents were not.

Tiggy cycled past the familiar homes; Harry 'Flash' Dobson's new housekeeper was sweeping the doorstep. Beryl was one of Alicia's latest recruits: outwardly chatty and caring but inwardly cold and calculating. She claimed a supernatural link to Harry's late wife in 'a Beryl takes all' bid to inherit. How Beryl had regretted having one too many Chardonnays and confiding her slippery scheme to Alicia. She had given Alicia power over her and would now do anything that Alicia asked.

When Tiggy arrived, Arthur Ramsbottom was reading the newspaper in his conservatory.

'I've gotta new housemate!' Tiggy told him, giving Arthur's hand a squeeze. 'An American baseball nut called Todd. You must meet him.'

'And is Todd single?'

'You're as bad as my mum. Yes, Todd is single!'

Arthur grinned, having often been an ear for Tiggy's relationship dramas. 'Just want you to be happy.'

'I am. He's just what I need right now, someone nice and uncomplicated,' Tiggy said without the faintest idea of how wrong she was.

'You mean after Gav?' Arthur asked.

'Yeah, a fresh start.' The old man could see the bad memory cogs turning in Tiggy's head.

'There's plenty more fish, and they're not all sharks,' Arthur added, 'and they're not all Gavs either.'

Tiggy nodded, looking thoughtful.

'I've told Todd that he can set up a baseball club. He wants to start a league.'

Arthur Ramsbottom's face dropped. 'Haven't you heard?'

'About Alicia's lot trying to shut us down?' Tiggy asked.

Arthur shook his head, his expression conveying something serious.

'She's not the problem, but this might be,' he said, flicking through his newspaper until he came to a particular page and reading the headline aloud.

'New Road and Housing set for Curse Village.'

'What's this?' Tiggy asked, skimming the article: a proposal for a housing development of 200 starter homes and a new road on the village outskirts that had had the first stage of plans passed.

'My drinking pal's daughter works in the Highways Department; she's seen a map of the affected area. The road will be coming right through your land and the houses on the edge of it. It'll be curtains for the track and ECM.'

'Is that legal?' Tiggy asked, looking alarmed.

'If they pass the plans, there won't be much you can do about it,' Arthur said, looking upset to be the one to break the news. He stroked Buddy's grey chin; the gentle, loyal Labrador was getting on in years, but he still lapped up the attention like a puppy.

'I'm gonna stop it somehow!' Tiggy said, punching a cushion in frustration, thinking about the children, the therapy animals, and her aspiring champions.

'They're saying the Lightning Tree will need to go,' Arthur added. Buddy sensed that he was upset and nuzzled his head into him.

Tiggy knew how much the tree meant to Arthur. It was his only tangible link to his brother Arnold.

'I won't let them, and I don't think Arnold will either,' she said, reflecting on the character of the Wobniar, who she had met on her rainbow journey.

Arthur shook his head. 'I'm not sure even Arnold and the powers he wields can stop an officious 'more than my job's worth council' on the promise of a bonus and a tasty backhander from the housing developers.' He frowned, his voice tinged with philosophical sadness. 'It's the way of the world,' he said, 'it's the way of the world.'

Chapter 10

THE RELEASE

I t was the first day in Todd's new home, and seeing his blue rainbow stone on Tiggy's mantelpiece as an innocent and harmless ornament had taken him back to the rainbow. His haunted face told the story of how he was a prisoner in the Indigo many moons before. He wanted to rid himself of the dark clouds and move forward freely, having finally arrived where he wanted his future to be; he would doctor his past by the present and put paid to his demons for good.

Todd took out a pen and began to write, reading aloud as each word took its place on the paper.

'When the Sacred Stone's door slid open and I watched Tiggy disappear into the golden light of the Rainbow's End it was the scariest moment of my life, knowing that I would be facing the terrors of the Indigo alone. Sometimes, the worst brings out the best in people, but I was a shaking wretch. How I wished my father would swoop in and scoop me up in his arms as he did when I was a child, or for my mother to tell me that everything would be fine. I could hear her soft, comforting voice, but she wasn't there. Nobody was. Stranded on an island within the stinking sewer of the swamp, I curled up small to hide from danger. I remember my fear and desperation from knowing I was at the mercy of the deadly Ogidni: the hideous serpent had already struck me once with its lethal, black slime. My numb body was failing, struggling to anchor my jellied limbs from toppling into the swamp. How much of it was from fear or the Ogidni's poison was uncertain, but what was clear was my helplessness in this moment. The Indigo's black, toxic energy invaded every pore, my dreads wet with sweat, sticking to my skin. I knew that there could be no escape, and it was only a matter of time before one of the serpent's seven deadly heads would lunge out of the murky light to inject its lethal cocktail, condemning me to the unknown fate of other failed Rainbow Children. Yet, within the confusion, came realisation: maybe this was why children sometimes randomly disappear without trace or warning. Was I to become another? I can still smell the putrid, rotting fleshy stench and hear the terrifying sounds: wailing and screaming from the Doom Tombs and the predatory slurps of a Dreamstealer circling overhead. How that ghastly noise penetrated and chilled me to the bone, even now it still deafens and haunts me in my sleep. Yet, with every acrid breath, my mother's hopeful words were tripping through my head on repeat, 'It's not over 'til it's over, Todd Bod'. She was a strong and optimistic force, always saying it when things were black and bleak. I so wanted her as I waited for a miracle. A flood of memories and thoughts of loved ones rushed in; a drowning realisation that I would never see their shining faces or hug them ever again. I had let them down. This was not the happy life story I imagined as a small child, beginning back home in the States, embroidering each later chapter there. There wasn't a single white picket fence and happy ending in sight— just this horror story. It seemed that nothing could save me, but my mother, as often before, was right: 'It's not over 'til it's over,' and whilst I prayed for a miracle, the unexpected happened: an inexplicable, extraordinary intervention, like a divine vision:

The Guardian of the Rainbow, the Wobniar, appeared with the Book of the Realms and a 'Vow of Secrecy'. The book was open, illuminating the page and offering a lifeline. I was trembling, my heartbeat thumping in my chest, realising that this would be my only chance. I studied the words, repeatedly reading the vow until the book closed:

When you leave beneath her angel wings,
Seraphina will fly you free,
She has made the ultimate sacrifice: her immortality.
Her wings she must relinquish,
Her celestial powers extinguish.
Seraphina puts her trust in you
To sustain her with 'The Power of Two ';
Let her drink in the rain, breathe in the sunshine,
These daily blessings are her earthly lifeline.
Without sunshine and rain, her eyes will close,
At this moment, your freedom froze.
You must both return as you first came
So, her celestial wings she may regain,
Her angel powers to restore
That she may live forevermore.
Alas, take note: whoever is Seraphina's final keeper
Their soul passes to 'The Grim Reaper'.
For when darkness falls through eyes closed tight
Only the rainbow can cast new light:
Angel Seraphina must come home,
This ultimate power is yours alone.
From the rainbow to the Lightning Tree,
I am the guardian of your destiny.

As I finished reading the message in the Book of the Realms for the final time, Angel Seraphina suddenly appeared in the Indigo, where the angels never ventured. She wrapped her wings around my feeble body, and I at once felt safe and protected by her celestial shield. I listened to the Wobniar's final parting words, repeating the vow to remember them.

'You are her lifeline, and she is yours. Never forget The Power of Two,' he said, flashing his sabre over us. I believe that in that moment he blessed us on our way. It was the most incredible feeling and change of fortune. Angel Seraphina had come to the rescue, and finally, I was going home. I shall never forget when we arrived, watching her wings shrivel and her light begin to fade as she diminished into a shadow of the angel she was. It was horrible. Seraphina had sacrificed her wings and celestial powers, trusting that I should be her earthly keeper. I am forever in her debt and pledged to take care of her through the good days and the bad.'

Todd stared at the paper, mulling over the words he had written that meant so much and weighed so heavily. They took up so little room, and yet, for Todd in that moment, their worth would fill the oceans and outweigh the stars. He paused to reflect, lost in the language of the Indigo Realm until he was ready to speak:

'I wish to rid myself of past burdens by destroying all dark and destructive thoughts,' Todd declared in a masterful voice.

Todd scrunched up the paper, took out a match, struck it, and holding the flame to the paper, watched as it burned and shrivelled in the sink.

'I banish you and am letting go,' Todd said, watching the paper crinkle and blacken into fragments. There was power in releasing this negativity, and he hoped that, like the sceptic he was, it would work. Todd gazed into the embers as the flame fizzled out, hoping that by destroying the rainbow's curses, he had not destroyed its blessings too.

Chapter 11

EVERY CHILD MATTERS

It was an early Easter, and Tiggy, having bribed the children with an Egg Hunt at the end of an intensive 'Easter Camp' at the track, was free to wind down for a brief stretch and spend some time getting to know her new housemate.

'Here!' Tiggy said, pointing to a vast area of grassy wasteland, 'flat as a pancake!'

Todd beamed. It was the perfect site for his baseball centre.

'Gee! You were always generous, um, I mean, you are so generous,' said Todd, stumbling over his words to correct himself, forgetting that Tiggy was clueless about their shared past and hoping he had got away with it.

Tiggy grinned. Todd's gaff hadn't registered; all she knew was that she felt the happiest she had in ages.

The Easter break was a busy time at 'Every Child Matters,' known to the locals as ECM. With time off school, the centre was a go-to place for the usual faces to gather; lots of parents and children were attending the 'Get to know our pets' session'. A local Veterinary Nurse was introducing the parents and children to the best care advice and tips for the pets and giving a 'hands-on' guide to the various daily routines. The nurse encouraged the children to stroke the animals, and by the end of the afternoon, even the more reluctant amongst them were bobbing around wanting to help at the feeding stations and fetch fresh hay. Alex had bought most of the animals, in his words, to 'help weduce anxiety, bwing calm, and impwove social interwaction'. The miniature donkeys, ponies, guinea pigs, and rabbits had played a huge part in Every Child Matter's success story: they were pets but also therapy animals, working their magic by their gentle and accepting presence. Of course, docile and friendly Buddy did his bit, too. Everyone loved Buddy, and he gave it back. However, Buddy was not ECM's only canine companion for the children to stroke and cuddle because Nureyev, a gentle-natured greyhound, had recently joined the ageing Labrador; he was a rescue dog, a leggy, whirlwind of energy never far from Penelope's side.

'Buddy should be on the payroll,' Tiggy joked as a swarm of children ran over to stroke him.

'Is he your boyfriend?' Daisy asked, pointing deliberately at Todd. Daisy was 10 but was young for her age. She was nosy and direct, but sometimes too personal and probing.

'Todd's my new housemate,' Tiggy replied, grinning at Todd and knowing that Daisy was likely to have more questions.

'He could be your boyfriend, though. Did you dump Gavin Peacock, or did he dump you? Daisy asked. 'He had big ears!' but distracted by Todd's red holdall, she didn't wait for Tiggy to reply. 'What's in your bag?' she enquired, trying to grab it.

'Just stuff!' Todd replied, manoeuvring the holdall away from her and swinging the bag onto his shoulder.

'Stuff!' Daisy repeated. 'Sounds like, 'Stuff and nonsense!'' and she skipped away giggling, having also made Todd laugh.

'I'll introduce you to Theo, Pen's new l'il bro'-in-law,' Tiggy said, calling to a short, squat boy feeding grass to a sweet, whisky coloured pony called 'Dewdrop.' However, Theo was so engrossed gathering up the fresh grass, he pretended not to hear. When Theo was on task, nothing and nobody got in his way; his brain was constantly overthinking inside its prison walls. Simon was nearby, showing Snowdrop, the white Falabella pony, his Rubik's cube. He was 13 and a couple of years older than Theo, but both boys had professor-like wisdom.

'Si is super smart with dates—calendar dates, not the awkward sort you go out on,' Tiggy said, trying to get Simon's attention. Todd grinned; she had often amused him in the rainbow. 'Give Si any date from the past, present, or future and he'll tell you the day of the week it is. He's never wrong.'

Todd raised his eyebrows, watching as Simon chatted to Snowdrop. He was tall for his age and towered over the cute little pony, but otherwise looked like an ordinary, regular young teen despite being inwardly extraordinary. There was no hiding it: Simon was telling the snowy white pony the current times for cities across different world time zones whilst twisting his cube behind his back and successfully completing it. ECM's jigsaw puzzle presented a happy scene today, and Simon was just one of its unfinished pieces looking to find his place: children who seldom joined in with others, and avoided close contact, were caring for the animals as if it was something they naturally wanted to do. The animals were the unwitting puzzle solvers, a bridge between the children and this foreign land of feelings.

'Hey Si!' Tiggy called out, walking towards a mop of auburn hair, the boy's most striking feature.

Simon half turned to look at them, his thick, tousled hair hiding his gorgeous, grey-green eyes that would never look at anybody for longer than he could help.

'My friend Todd,' she said, gesturing to him, 'wants to know what day of the week Christmas Day was in 1976?'

'In 1976, it was a Saturday.' Simon didn't even need to think about it. There was no expression on his face or emotion in his voice for his robot-like response.

'Thanks Dude!' Todd said, putting his fist out to bump it with Simon's, but he was twisting his cube again.

'You're welcome!' Simon fired back, not looking up.

Tiggy knew that Simon was right: it was the year that her life-changing rainbow adventures had lifted the village's killer curse.

'Gee, Dude! That's what I call 'serious skills!' Todd remarked, but Simon had already turned his back.

'You must meet ECM's 'Mini Einstein,' Theo. He's like my brother Alex, their superpower is scientific,' she said, walking towards the converted barn and premises of Every Child Matters. 'C'mon, Buddy! Let's show Todd around.'

The converted barn was an impressive renovation of high beamed ceilings, glazed windows and open spaces, full of character with magnificent views in all directions, particularly from the stunning galleried landing, the home of ECM's creative displays and works of art:

murals, mosaics and sculptures, drawings, paintings and poetry of variable artistic merit but each wonderful in its own way.

'All the kids work,' Tiggy said, pointing to various pieces on the galleried landing. 'I never knew you could do so much with squeezy bottles and egg cartons!' she joked, pointing out some models using all manner of unusual and imaginative materials.

'Looks like a Degas,' Todd said, admiring a sculpture of an elegant ballet dancer standing on a nearby shelf and illuminated beneath a spotlight.

'Solomon spent hours sculpting it from sketches he made watching Pen dance. Solomon's a bit obsessed with Pen, but in a nice, not creepy, way.'

'It's pretty awesome!' Todd said, marvelling how the boy had captured the ballerina's graceful posture and movement from the lump of moulded clay.

'Of course, they're not all Einsteins and Picassos!' She bent down to pick up some Lego bricks scattered across the floor. 'I see them as human conundrums with different wiring and invisible stuff going on: for instance, Solomon, who made the ballet dancer, can do that, but he can't speak. People stare at him like he's rude, but it's not that. They get him wrong 'cos he's different.'

'You'd never know,' Todd said, picking up another stray brick.

'It's hidden just like superpowers,' Tiggy said, leading him into a small room full of Lego building tables, each storing an assortment of coloured blocks. 'This stuff usually keeps things calm.' Tiggy pointed to a tall tower of Lego bricks, 'a lot of the kids really like it.'

Four children were working together at a table on an original design. A boy called Harry was the 'Engineer,' Sophie and Grace, the 'Builders,' and Leeroy, the 'Supplier'. Harry's dad, Nick, was supervising to ensure 'fair play', but none of them took charge, the children finding a hidden power from the little bricks to cooperate with one another without saying much.

'How's it going?' Tiggy asked.

'Fine up to now, but we lost Toby and Eli early doors,' Nick replied, 'Toby wanted to build Tower Bridge, but these guys outvoted him.'

'He always builds Tower Bridge,' mumbled Leeroy without looking up, sorting the bricks into colours.

'Yes, Toby's very fond of Tower Bridge,' Tiggy agreed, knowing that Leeroy was right. Toby repeatedly built the bridge and demolished other constructions that were not a fit, and his little brother Eli helped him do it.

The distant keys of someone playing a piano were coming from the studio where Penelope was taking a class. Tiggy smiled. 'You're in for a treat,' she said, following Buddy, who was leading the way; he'd often go there to meet up with Nureyev. They peeped through the glass. The children, wearing ECM's black and gold tops, were in full flow. Angelica, who was 12 and obsessively snacked on blueberries, was playing Mrs. Derbyshire's old piano. Her agile fingers confidently stroked the keys with a flamboyant fluency as she felt the music. Anyone watching saw a child with her eyes closed, and body swaying, fully immersed as she executed the piece with light and shade, soft touch and mesmeric power. Such a showy performance made it difficult to believe that she was an introverted girl who preferred to eat her blueberries alone.

'I could listen to Angelica all day long,' Tiggy said, smiling at Blessings who was sitting cross-legged stroking Nureyev, his legs splayed, asleep on his back in his dog bed. The children were in 'free movement', interpreting the music in their own way. Suddenly, Blessings, who was slightly younger than Angelica, got up and started to sing. Her pure, pitch-perfect voice was like warm honey: smooth and sweet with a rich, distinctive flavour.

'Pen calls her, 'their nightingale!' Tiggy said, opening the studio door. Buddy ambled in and slumped down next to Nureyev, who was like a fixture whenever the children danced. Retired from racing and discarded, Penelope had rescued the sweet-natured greyhound and given him his forever home. Looking at him on his back, contented and soundly sleeping, his harsh and competitive background was hard to believe. He was a gentle soul, and the children loved it when Nureyev watched them dance.

Not all the children were natural movers, but they did what they could and with enthusiasm, dancing around Jessie Jennings, a dainty little girl, sat in the middle of the floor. Her caramel hair lovingly arranged into such a neat, slick bun made it seem even more of a pity that she wasn't joining in. She did sometimes. However, some of the children were graceful, expressive, and intentional as they danced, and one child stood out: his movement had authority with perfect lines, poise, and artistry beyond the ordinary.

'That's Omari,' Tiggy whispered discreetly, gesturing as an athletic, distinctive-looking boy glissade past them. He looked lean enough to snap in two, but there was huge strength in his sinewy, conditioned body, and his charismatic display of technique and musicality was unchallenged, wrapped up in Omari's very own brand of magic.

'Now you can see what a witch Alicia Gold is for wanting to close us down,' Tiggy said as he completed a series of perfect pirouettes in front of them as though glued to the spot. 'The kids are no more dangerous than I am!'

Later, when they were on their way out, Solomon and his mother, Tanisha, had just arrived with a new piece of work fresh off Solomon's easel to pin up in his personal section on ECM's 'Wall of Fame'. His Easter treat of a trip to London had afterwards resulted in his inked watercolour of the London skyline. Every geometrical detail was perfect and precise. He had not needed to see the sunrise to produce his glowing and breathtaking version of a 'St Paul's at sunrise' worthy of hanging in any gallery.

'It's brilliant!' Tiggy said, staring at the picture and smiling at Solomon, but he didn't look at her.

'He wouldn't eat his food until it was on the wall,' Tanisha replied.

Tiggy looked at the heavy bags under Tanisha's dark eyes. She looked weary. There were many rewards, but it was also draining having a Solomon in your life.

'Todd here,' she said, gesturing to her housemate to introduce him, 'has been admiring your ballerina sculpture.'

'I'm in awe, Dude,' Todd said, looking for a reaction.

Solomon was silent, his head down, but he had heard every word.

Outside, Alicia and her mob were starting their daily protest at ECM's peak hour for traffic. They wanted to have maximum impact for minimum time.

'What do we need?' Alicia shouted.

'Shut down!' the mob responded.

Solomon looked anxious, tugging on his mother's arm to go. With his new picture in place now perhaps he would eat, but not if Alicia and her noisy gang had their way.

'They were gathering when we arrived, wanting to intimidate. They tried to block our way, shouting at us when we passed,' Tanisha said, putting her arm around her son. Todd shook his head in disbelief. 'Solomon hates it, and I'm worried he'll want to stop coming here.'

Tiggy put a sympathetic hand on Tanisha's shoulder, 'What brutes!' she said as Solomon tugged again on his mother's arm.

'It's good to meet you, Dude!' Todd said, holding out his hand for Solomon to shake.

The boy looked up and stared at Todd, first at his face and then his chest, gazing with such an unnerving intensity that it was as if he wanted to penetrate his soul. It was for an uncomfortable length of time, and Todd's hand was still waiting.

'Solomon? Are you ready to go?' Tanisha asked, trying to bring her son back to her. He was in his own bubble, in 'Solomon's world', unaware of anyone or anything except for a universe of thoughts in his head, there and yet on another level, he was somewhere else. Solomon kept staring at Todd long after he had retracted his hand. 'Solomon!' his mother repeated, trying to break through.

Suddenly, the boy banged his hand three times on his mother's bag. Without words or any visible communication, she passed him a sketchpad and a tin of artist's pens and, flipping it open, he started drawing with a frenzied attack of coloured ink upon the page.

'Just when I thought we were about to go!' Tanisha said, hoping that Solomon's rude staring hadn't spooked Todd.

'So, how was London?' Tiggy enquired.

Tanisha hesitated and nodded a few times, her eyes diverted, stalling for thinking time.

'Fine thanks! London's still standing!' she said, but it was more what she didn't say.

Solomon continued to draw with a fervour and purpose until the final flourish of his pen. He tore the sheet from his pad, folded and handed it to his mother, and pointed to Todd. Tanisha peeped inside the folded paper, raising her eyebrows.

'Solomon wants you to have it,' she said, passing it to Todd, 'but look at it later...that's why it's folded.'

Solomon bowed his head.

'Now perhaps we'll get to eat!' Tanisha quipped, 'Please tell Miss Penelope we've been,' and linking arms with her son, they left.

Todd watched them from the window swerve around Alicia's baying group, as Solomon, now with his hands over his ears, hurried past.

'I've really no words!' Todd exclaimed, disgusted by the scene outside.

'And neither has Solomon,' responded Tiggy in acknowledgement of Solomon, the non-speaking savant.

Chapter 12

THE MYSTERY HOLDALL

The next morning, Penelope knocked at Tiggy's door.

'There's no need to knock Mrs Green!' Tiggy called out as Penelope rushed in with Nureyev, looking flushed and flustered.

'Is the honeymoon over already?' Tiggy cheeked.

Penelope smirked, 'Well, it is, but not in the married sense. I've just come from Mum's...she reckons they're defo going to close us down.' She looked grave and close to tears.

'Who's to blame, Alicia or the Council?' Tiggy asked, her mind spinning, knowing that Arthur Ramsbottom thought so, too.

'The Council: they've approved the first stage of plans for a major new road and housing estate. Mum has a letter about compo to move. It's a pittance!' Penelope said.

'I'll never afford to re-open. As if I can move my track. This stinks!' Tiggy growled.

'Yeah, that's what Mum said. It'll finish us,' Penelope agreed.

'The thought of Alicia getting her way and poor Arthur losing the Lightning Tree,' Tiggy added, looking upset.

'Um, not sure she'll be happy either though,' Penelope said with such composure that Tiggy instantly felt calmer. 'It will affect her too...a busy road, hundreds of homes, and the massacre of all the trees, not just the Lightning Tree. Trust me! She isn't going to be happy.'

On days off, Todd was usually a late riser, but the girls' impassioned chat woke him. He still had Solomon's neatly folded picture in his pocket.

'Gee!' Todd whispered under his breath, staring at Solomon's brilliant composition. His rainbow journey was in front of him, drawn in detail: the Wobniar on his crystal throne, surrounded by rainbow angels. Did Solomon have the power to see right through him and into the past? Could he see his life's path and troubled journey to be where he was right now?

Todd listened at the door. The sisters were talking about Gav deserving to be her ex.

'He hadn't changed a bit,' Tiggy moaned, 'he'd been playing us both.'

'Move on, sister!' Penelope said with a sassy 'Boss bitch' tone, 'Nobody thought you and Gav were a good idea. Not even Mr R.'

'I've been a fool!' Tiggy agreed.

'What d'ya think of your new housemate?' Penelope asked, grinning, 'I've heard good things. I thought he sounded like your type.'

'Maybe on paper, but I need to get to know him. He seems cool though.'

'Shame I had a class yesterday when you called, I thought you might introduce us. Rachel Harris described him as the 'hottest hunk' since Take That!'

'She would!' Tiggy said, adopting a neutral manner since she had never been a fan of the boy band, or any other. 'He is possibly on my radar, though.'

Todd was still eavesdropping, unsure what to think about the Take That comparison, but he was happy to hear that he was 'possibly' on her 'radar'. The years of longing to see the vibrant girl again he had first met in the rainbow, was building into something more.

'What's in the holdall?' Penelope asked.

'Dunno! He's always got it with him.'

Todd looked at the innocent-looking bag, feeling anxious that it was a talking point.

'The Power of Two!' he mumbled, opening the window.

After heavy rainfall overnight, raindrops were like glistening globules on the window's varnished ledge. Todd soaked them up with his hanky.

'Nourishment time,' he whispered, staring into his bag at a garland of sunflowers and dabbing the largest flower's face with his hanky. He moved the holdall onto the sill to soak up the early spring sunshine streaming through the open window. Angel Seraphina stared back at him from the flower's rich brown centre; the sunflowers were shining bright, and so, too, were Angel Seraphina's eyes.

'Rain and sunshine, The Power of Two' he said, 'I promise, my Angel, to keep you safe.'

Suddenly, there was a knock on his bedroom door.

'Come and meet Mrs Green. She's dying to meet you!' Tiggy called outside the door, amused to use Penelope's married name. She had no idea about the surge of panic that she had triggered inside the room.

'I'll be back,' he whispered to his angel and zipping up his holdall, he hid it beneath his bed.

Just as with Tiggy, Todd's connection with Penelope was instant, and although they were all quite different characters, the trio hit it off and the chat was easy.

'You surprise me,' Penelope said, staring and smiling at Todd, 'To be honest, I thought you'd be cocky and annoying.'

'Oh dear, do I give those vibes?' Todd asked, a bit taken aback and stroking Buddy for extra thinking time.

'Noooo!' It's just that anyone Tig brings home is usually like that, especially her last one!'

Tiggy was indignant. 'Pen! You're making me sound like an awful judge of character!'

'Well, you sort of are where men are concerned,' retorted Penelope.

Tiggy hesitated, 'Um yeah! Gav was cocky and annoying, and he had big ears!' she concluded as they all burst out laughing.

'Who's that? Are you expecting anyone?' Penelope asked, hearing a car pull up outside and seeing a flash of movement through the window. Tiggy shrugged, glancing from behind the curtains.

'Ergh! It's Rach Harris's car!' Tiggy groaned, expecting it to be about Bo, her club's newest member, having not long started at the track. Rach, wearing a 'Take That,' cap was staring in through the window, having a good old nose before knocking.

'Just to let you know,' Rach began still trying to peer inside when Tiggy opened the door, 'Bo will be here on Wednesday. Also, please don't tell Alicia that Bo trains with you.'

'Okay, as usual then,' Tiggy replied, puzzled that Rach had felt the need to call and tell her. It seemed like an excuse, and she was still staring, trying to look around corners as if she were looking for something or someone. She was. Rach was after Todd.

'Hope you don't mind but the VW campervan…just wondered if you'd be interested in selling?'

'It's my housemate's,' Tiggy replied. Rach had irritated her, suspecting that the enquiry wasn't genuine. She was staring indoors and looking everywhere but at Tiggy.

'Would that be the dishy guy with the cute hat and holdall? I've heard rumblings that he's living here.'

'He is, but he's not in!'

Tiggy just wanted rid of her, suspecting that Todd would be grateful for keeping Raunchy Rach at bay.

'Aw, shame!' Rach continued, undeterred by Tiggy's blunt manner. 'P'raps you'd give him this please,' she said, handing Tiggy a note with her telephone number and an invitation to call her. 'It's about the campervan, although I wouldn't mind seeing what he's got in his holdall!' Rach said with a hen night cackle that made Todd, who was nearby listening in, shudder. He was a newcomer with a secret, and nobody could or would ever know what was in his holdall, and certainly not Raunchy Rach.

Chapter 13

THE TWINS

'Gather round!' Tiggy called out to eight of her most talented and dedicated young riders. This was the 'Elite Squad' her 'the chosen ones' she expected to trade their commitment and hard work for more coaching and track time. Mikey Junior and Michaela hadn't made it to training. She wasn't surprised, just disappointed: the twins' talent promised much, but it would be a hollow talent if they were never there. A middle-aged man and a younger woman dressed in cosy casuals and caps were hovering nearby with a clipboard. The children stared at them, wondering what these unlikely-looking cyclists were doing there.

'We're working on hard and fast today, winning those gates and finishes,' Tiggy said. 'With UK Champs coming up, I'm looking for great starts at every gate.' The children nodded; they all wanted to win. Tiggy looked across at the strangers. 'We've two movie scouts with us today who'll be watching you.' Tiggy gave them a nod. 'Over to you guys!'

The man and woman introduced themselves. They were casting directors, seeking two young riders for a feature film with a tasty pay cheque attached.

Suki and Laura's eyes were alight. They wanted this and would do whatever it took to get it, at once trying to smile and catch the casting crew's attention by doing cartwheels in front of them.

'Just do what you'd usually do, kids. No acting for now, we just want to see you in action,' the man said as the woman pinned a number to each child's top, taking down their name.

Suddenly, a battered Ford Escort screeched to a halt several metres away, overshooting the car park. Mikey Junior and Michaela tumbled out of the back door, helmets already fastened and ready to go. Tiggy waved at Mikey, aware of the effort involved for the twins to be there. Mikey had undoubtedly sacrificed sleeping before being back on shift again.

'What's the film called?' a sandy-haired lad called Scotty asked, his eyes shining with imagined Hollywood fame.

'BMX Baby' but it's just a working title for now, so it could change further down the track.'

Scotty was a Scot called Scott, and Mikey Junior's main male rival (although Robbo, Ed and Sid would have disputed it) whilst Michaela on her day, could beat them all.

'I ain't no baby!' Scotty muttered loud enough for the casting directors to hear. They made a note of his number.

'Okay, Scotty! You can show them on the track. Starting gates everyone!' Tiggy ordered. Robbo, a small lad for his age but with a big personality, dragged his feet on the ground. 'I need more from you this session. Don't be intimidated 'cos they're bigger than you, just believe in your talent and commit,' Tiggy instructed as Robbo passed her.

'You got it!' Robbo said with a cheeky wink that made the casting directors smile.

The children cycled away, charged up, and raring to go. Tiggy watched the pack eagle-eyed, taking in the positives and negatives for each rider's performance. They were on fire, hungry to impress the casting directors, who were scribbling down notes and whispering to each other, but were impossible to read. After several gates, Tiggy called the group back. She was hopeful that she had a future UK champion and even possible film stars amongst them.

'So, what are the 3 key areas we need to be better than anyone else?' Tiggy asked. A host of enthusiastic hands shot up into the air. They all knew the answer, but MJ shouted it out.

'Stance, Ming, and Snap, Miss.'

'Yes MJ!' Tiggy said, noticing the casting directors were looking deadpan at the twins.

'Gotta be alert though, Miss,' Micky called out, not wanting her twin to outshine her. MJ rolled his eyes, and the casting directors glanced at one another.

'That's right, Micky! Be alert and be present! Gates everyone!'

Suddenly, screeching brakes and a honking car horn disrupted the group's focus. All heads looked across at the car park, Tiggy half expecting to see Mikey back again. However, this time it was the twins' mother, Sapphire, hoping not to have to get out of the car. The twins ignored it, heading for the starting gates. Sapphire, with a face like thunder and her baby in her arms, marched over to the track.

'I need the twins!' she said to Tiggy and staring at the casting directors, 'What's the idiot doing dropping them here. I told him I'm out tonight!'

'Now!' Sapphire ordered, with a savage look on her immaculately made-up face.

'But Mum! They're film people!' MJ said, undoing his helmet.

'Now!' she repeated, 'You can tell me in the car.'

The twins looked gutted, bundling themselves into the back of the car, the door only just closed before she sped away. Tiggy felt sorry for the twins, but the casting directors were asking questions about them and left shortly afterwards, having seen enough.

The last few minutes of the training session remained when Alicia and her mob arrived to start their protest. Tiggy broke.

'Are you still hounding innocent children?' she snapped. 'Haven't you heard about the new road and planned development?'

'Of course, but it won't affect me!' a misinformed Alicia replied.

'It most certainly will affect you. You're batting for the wrong side! Jog on!' Tiggy looked disgusted.

'What does she mean?' Alicia asked her group, confusion written all over her hard-looking face.

'D'ya mean about the 'innocent children'?' Beryl asked, not having kept up.

Alicia rolled her eyes, 'Where's Hugo when he's needed? He has questions to answer!' She looked rattled, 'Protest over for tonight! I need to get to the bottom of this!' and she stomped away with her cronies close on her heels.

Casting directors and Alicia aside, Tiggy continued working her group hard, determined to squeeze the most out of the session.

'Let's have some explosive power to finish!' she yelled, noticing the parents were already back again to collect. If the children were competitive with each other, the parents were, too, always watching and waiting to see who received the session's 'star rider' from Tiggy. Today Suki received the special congratulatory handshake. The children all wanted it, but only one would get it, disappointing the parents when their child missed out. Unbeknown to everybody, the series of claps and hand slaps in all directions was in fact, the 'Special Buddy' she and the Stig Man had invented in the rainbow, making the handshake in Tiggy's mind, a greater award than anyone could ever imagine.

'School, track, rest, repeat! See you tomorrow!' Tiggy called out as they were leaving.

She wandered across to the office, unable to get the proposed new road and development out of her mind. How could a few starchy men and women in suits with nothing better to do snatch all this away as if it didn't matter? She pinned her session's feedback, complete with her 'star rider' onto the 'This week In Training' notice board, locking the door behind her.

In the fading light, Mikey had arrived to collect the twins.

'Mum's already taken them!' Tiggy told him, 'She was none too happy, so watch out!'

'They'll be minding the sprog! It's the only reason she wanted them.' Mikey looked miffed and miserable.

Tiggy felt sorry for them; it was neither right nor legal, but to date, Social Services were only aware of the twins' late and haphazard attendance at school. Mikey's cheeky spark from his 'wild child' days was gone, and nowadays he looked haggard and hassled, but he loved the twins and tried to be a good dad. Tiggy felt awful, drowning in guilt because Mikey had been at the Speed House-mating event, and she, like everyone else that night, because of his unsociable hour shifts and difficult domestic arrangements, had decided he wasn't a suitable match. He also came with boisterous twins who were a lot to handle.

'Are you still looking for a place to stay?' Tiggy asked, suspecting he had been sleeping in his car.

Mikey nodded. 'Sapph's moving her new fella in. I can't keep sofa surfing at my mate's; he's given me 'til the weekend.'

Tiggy wasn't sure whether to believe him about his mate's. The inside of the car looked like a makeshift bedroom with a quilt and pillows catching her eye. She paused to ponder. This was the 'new Mikey', a father of twins and clearly down on his luck. Sapphire had been the one who had cheated. Nevertheless, he had bullied Alex and crushed his confidence all those years ago. It was such a stark contrast and change of character. Could she, and should she, forgive his past? The tables had turned: Alex, the nerdy, uncool outsider at school was now one of the hottest rising stars and insiders at NASA, whilst Mikey, the coolest cat in high school was now a night owl stacking supermarket shelves and although a steady, honest living, it certainly did not light up his world.

'I've got a spare room. You could stay at mine 'til UK Champs, and we can see how it goes?' Tiggy said, feeling her guilty burden shift. 'It's easier for the track when you've got the twins, provided they can sofa surf.'

Mikey smiled the biggest smile Tiggy had seen on his face in many a long month.

Chapter 14

THE U-TURN

'What's up, Uppers? Do spill before that cravat chokes you!' Alicia quipped to the village's 'Man in the Know', her piercing eyes burning into his neatly tied scarlet cravat. She knew that he never wore red for 'Routine Thursdays' and it was Hugo F. Uppingham's 'crisis colour' signalling an 'emergency meeting' of major importance.

'Patience, Mrs Gold! I shall reveal all once everyone is here,' he said, turning his back, peeved by her mocking. Nobody, not even Alicia Gold, spoke down to Hugo Uppingham.

Rach arrived and at once distanced herself from Alicia by being unusually friendly to Gertie Grimshaw, who was greeting everyone from her wheelchair with her gnome of the moment on her lap. Her daughter Bo's attendance at BMX Mania was such a betrayal to Alicia, who was hell bent on closing the place down.

'Come!' Alicia beckoned to Rach, patting the seat next to her. Rach couldn't refuse her; Alicia knew sensitive information about Bo's real father, and it was not the man who Bo called 'Dad.' Alicia could be brutal when triggered, and so Rach, having accepted the seat, removed her 'Take That' cap to redo her ponytail and avoid eye contact.

'Could I take that?' Timothy enquired, referring to Rach's boy band cap that had fallen onto the floor.

Rach giggled, 'Could you 'take that?' You! Be in a boy band?' she mocked, 'Soz Mr G, it ain't personal but with respect, you just ain't gonna cut it!'

Alicia looked perplexed, 'I can see this is going to be a long and tiring morning. Hugo, just spit it out!'

Silence fell upon the room. Alicia was so rude.

'It saddens me to be the bearer of bad news,' Hugo Uppingham began, staring at a room of anxious faces. Terence Tiddy started to choke on his shortbread, causing Hugo to pause whilst Ernest McAvey patted his partner's back.

'There, there!' Ernest said, 'Any better?'

Terence continued to splutter, his hamster cheeks turning beetroot until Beryl passed him her water bottle to sip.

'Betterish!' Terence whispered.

Alicia scowled, 'For goodness' sake, in future leave the shortbread at home! Can we get back to it?'

Hugo cleared his throat, 'Got a bit of a frog,' he said, stroking his cravat.

'I haven't got all day!' Alicia reminded him, checking her gold diamond-encrusted watch.

'A tickle?' Terence enquired, 'It sounds sort of ticklish.'

'No, it's more of a frog,' said Hugo, popping a throat lozenge into his mouth.

Alicia pointedly looked at her watch again and Hugo got the message.

'Now back to business!' he resumed, 'The council has approved a late tweak to the plans for the new road, and housing development that originally wouldn't have affected us.' Hugo scanned the room's shocked faces, sucking noisily on his lozenge.

'But will it affect me?' Alicia enquired.

'It most certainly will!' Hugo confirmed, 'and you, in particular, Alicia, being on the cusp of Heavenly Gardens.'

'This can't be right! Do they know who I am?' Alicia complained as she paced the room.

'My dear friend, I've seen the map, and it will pass right by your front door, and through the Tipple's farmland,' Hugo said. He paused for Alicia to react. 'There'll also be a metropolis of shoebox starter homes on the meadows.'

'What a nightmare! Our beautiful village ruined!' Gertie Grimshaw exclaimed.

'We must oppose it!' her husband concluded, and everyone agreed, including Alicia still looking shocked.

'It makes all our protesting a complete waste of time. We need to show them what we're made of!' Alicia said, shaking her fist and jangling her charm bracelet. 'I'd happily settle for Simple Simon running amok with his father's chainsaw rather than this catastrophic proposition.'

'I was coming to that,' Hugo said with an upbeat tone, 'we've proved beyond any reasonable doubt how good we are at protesting, have we not? So my thoughts are to flip the protest.'

'Eh?' Beryl said, looking confused.

'Allow me to explain,' Hugo said, his eyes popping as he accidentally swallowed his lozenge. 'We need to use the things we've been fighting against as our power.'

'Eh?' Beryl repeated.

'You mean we need to join forces with BMX Mania and Every Child Matters?' Gertie asked, rocking her gnome.

'Spot on!' Hugo agreed, 'We protest that their significant and irreplaceable value, vital to the lifeblood of our community and others, would be lost.'

'Please tell me I'm dreaming!' Alicia muttered under her breath.

'We simply change our protest to 'Save our Track because Every Child Matters,' Hugo said, looking around to read the room.

'Ah, I get it!' Beryl said, nodding. 'That makes sense.'

'Good work, Uppers! I'd never have thought of that!' Rach added, giving him a clap.

Hugo looked smug. 'So do we all concur that stopping the construction of the new road and houses in our own backyards is our number one priority?'

Everyone agreed, including Alicia, 'I'll get the placards changed,' she said with an accepting grimace for the battle ahead.

Chapter 15

WHEN A LEOPARD CHANGES ITS SPOTS

The wheels of a dirty Ford Escort pulled up outside the Tipple's farmhouse. From now on, or at least for a trial period, this would be home, and things were looking up for the Tipples' former nemesis and thorn in the side, 'Mikey Mucus'. Tiggy would soon find out whether the leopard really had changed its spots. Nothing tells you more about a person than living with them: she hoped her instincts were right.

'I wasn't sure if the twins would be moving in with you,' Tiggy remarked as Mikey Junior and Michaela bombed past her with armfuls of 'can't live without' kids' stuff.

Mikey nodded. 'The ex is glad to get shot!' he said, lowering his voice so that the twins didn't hear.

'What about the baby?' Tiggy enquired, knowing how the twins were often its babysitters.

'Not my sprog, not my problem!' Mikey declared, the bitterness sounding in every syllable. 'She'll manage; she always does!' he added, bending to stroke Buddy, who was wagging his tail and contorting his body with great excitement. 'She's moving her new fella in and they're talking of hiring a nanny; he's minted by all accounts and owns a fancy home on the south coast. I reckon they'll move down there.'

'It's such a shame. You were always such a cool couple in school,' Tiggy said, seeing the sadness in his eyes betraying his tough exterior.

'I've got some air beds for the kids to kip on my floor rather than sofa surf in your lounge. That ain't fair on you.'

Tiggy nodded. Was this really the same Mikey who had had such a horrible reputation at school, now standing here being so considerate of others?

'Hey! Put it back!' Mikey called out to the twins playing 'catch' with Tiggy's friendship stone that they had spotted on the mantelpiece. Tiggy held out her hand to take it from them, hiding the panic she was feeling inside about her most precious possession.

'No touching stuff that's not yours!' Mikey instructed as Tiggy put the stone out of their reach. It was clear that Mikey had grown a respect for people and their things. He didn't have much: a bin bag of clothes and bedding, a wallet in his back jeans pocket, and his car was a cupboard for anything else.

'I've just seen old Arthur camped out by the curse tree.'

'The Lightning Tree?' Tiggy queried.

'Yeah, he's a bit old for camping.'

Tiggy had heard enough. 'You're in the first bedroom on the left. There's lagers in the fridge and lollies for the kids in the ice box at the top. Help yourselves and make yourself at home.'

'It's much appreciated,' Mikey called out as Tiggy rushed from the house, grabbing her bike.

After the curse's demise, Arthur Ramsbottom had often visited the Lightning Tree, but he certainly wasn't the camping-out type: even when he was younger, he always liked his home comforts and recliner chair. Tiggy sped along the track, veering around Todd's campervan loaded up with materials for the new baseball field. He was on her father's old ride-on mower, cutting the grass to prepare the field's surface. Nobody had used it since the day of the accident, the mower overturning and causing a fatal head injury. Seeing the mower looking so harmless, Tiggy felt sick in the pit of her stomach, but it wasn't Todd's fault. He'd switched out his bucket hat for a baseball cap, excited to be creating his dream. His red holdall sat on the newly cut diamond; it was never far from Todd.

Tiggy cycled on until she had the Lightning Tree in her sights. Mikey was right; next to a pop-up tent, Arthur Ramsbottom was sitting beneath the tree on a fold-up chair, blanket over his knees, nursing a small cool bag and flask. The silvery giant was a part of the village's history, and whether it was for good, when the curse went away, or for bad, when the storm's lightning first struck the tree and twin boys, it had put their village on the map.

'We won't let them cut it down, Mr R,' Tiggy said, trying to sound reassuring. Arthur looked so unusually sad, but she knew exactly why and the reason for the stakeout. 'If it can possibly make a difference, Mum says she'll turn down the compo. We will stop them!'

Tiggy poured him a drink from the flask, 'I'll top this up and bring you more supplies.'

Arthur sipped from the cup and nodded. Arthur was going nowhere.

'It'll be over my dead body!' Arthur exclaimed, and he meant it.

Tiggy stared at the bleached trunk, tracing her fingers over the carved messages just as she did as a 9-year-old visiting Mrs Derbyshire. She knew they belonged to Arthur and his twin, Arnold, who had mysteriously gone missing on the ill-fated night of the storm.

'Who was 'JD'?' she asked, her fingers roving across the inscriptions, 'AR & JD TRUE LOVE' and 'JD4AR.' 'Was she a girlfriend?'

Arthur's sombre face changed, and his lips started to curl upwards at the corners.

'Kind of. We were only 9, going on 10.'

'Was she yours or Arnold's?' Tiggy asked. She loved Arthur's trips down Memory Lane.

'Mine!' he replied, the twinkle returning to his eyes. 'Her name was Joan Dewhurst, 'my Dewy'. Dark ringlets, and the bluest eyes I've ever seen. All the boys liked Joan.'

'You had some competition then?'

'I most certainly did!' he paused, 'Arnold!'

Tiggy laughed, 'That's not 'Bro' Code!'

Arthur chuckled. 'She was my first kiss. It was walking home from school.'

Tiggy was pleased to have cheered him up, 'Good memories, eh?'

Arthur nodded. It was true: they were old but gold, taking him back to a time when he and his twin, Arnold, were inseparable: one mind, one heart, until Arnold wasn't there any longer. For years he felt that half of him was missing, ripped away in an instant. That was why this lonely tree with its distinctive jagged branches mattered. The 'Lightning Tree' was their tree, the last time that the two had been one.

Tiggy and Arthur reminisced until well into the afternoon, and as Tiggy made a move to fetch extra provisions from home, Alicia appeared with her entourage.

'Not that lot again!' Tiggy said, irritated at the sight of them. 'I thought they'd have quit trying to close us down. Surely, there's bigger fish to fry!'

She was right. Alicia had made a complete U-turn.

'Save our trees! Save our track, because 'Every Child Matters!' Alicia's gang chanted, marching past on the public right of way. It was as if Tiggy and Arthur weren't there. Onwards the protesters stomped, Alicia with her nose in the air, her jewellery glistening.

'Am I dreaming?' Tiggy asked. They burst out laughing at Alicia's ludicrous change of heart, watching them until out of shot.

On her way home, Tiggy passed Todd again, still hard at it, creating his new baseball field. It was coming on well; he had cut the grassy outfield, laid, and marked out the sandy clay infield, and was preparing to chalk more lines. Solomon was with him, trailing behind, carrying his red holdall. The twins, keen to explore their new surroundings had also rocked up and sat cross-legged at the edge of the markings, playing on their Game Boys whilst casting a cursory eye at Todd.

'Looks like some kinda weird pitch,' Mikey Junior commented to his sister.

'Um, maybe,' Michaela replied, not that interested, fixated on her game.

'He's following Todd,' Mikey said, watching Solomon, a pace or two behind, in Todd's steps.

Todd was pushing a chalking device, marking out more lines whilst chatting to Solomon, who looked to be listening but also uncharacteristically, not taking his eyes off him. The pair connected the first time they met at ECM, a bond that was continuing to grow from strength to strength. Solomon was fast becoming Todd's shadow.

'He looks cool to live with. Don't need his 'tag along' though! Todd's *our* housemate, so he can do one!' Mikey Junior muttered, his competitive streak rising to the fore.

Chapter 16

SOLOMON

A couple of weeks passed, and things ticked over without drama or complications. Todd had taken the twins under his wing when Mikey wasn't around, and whilst the bread, milk and hot water had often run out, Tiggy loved the 'full house vibe'. She was also growing closer and closer to Todd. A quick chat always turned into hours, and Mikey had noticed electricity between them.

'You two spark off each other well,' he commented to Tiggy, grabbing a coffee to keep him awake.

'D'ya reckon?' Tiggy asked, not confident about any man's feelings towards her.

'Yeah, it's obvious! Me and Sapph used to be like that,' Mikey said with regret and sadness etched upon his face. The truth was that Mikey still loved her, but in his mind, the relationship had crumbled because he wasn't good enough. Sapphire had big dreams; she wanted the flash cars, designer gear, and the yacht, and her natural beauty was the key to unlocking her fantasies. They were a love match at school and Mikey, her 'Mr Right', but now she wanted a 'Mr Right Wealthy'.

'That's sad! Choosing money over true love,' Tiggy concluded after Mikey had poured out his heart to her.

'She thinks she can have both, but she'll never have this again,' he said, touching his heart, 'I know what's real and what isn't.'

It seemed to Tiggy that Mikey's engine was at full throttle through his teenage years and burnt out by his twenties, but he had certainly grown up in the process and was a decent man and good father.

Every evening after a tough, focussed session at the track, the twins wandered down to the baseball field to see Todd. Solomon did, too; after spending time at ECM he always looked for Todd. The non-speaking teen had forged an inexplicable and unbreakable connection with him that made the twins jealous. They lived with Todd, so he was 'their Todd'. Solomon was an impostor.

It was Saturday evening, and the twins had been at the track all day. The UK Championships were getting closer, but so, too, was the baseball Club's grand opening.

A competition to give the club its name was attracting a lot of interest, and with every passing day, more people were becoming aware of Todd's plan to bring a slice of America to the village.

For a long time, Todd's campervan was full of mystery boxes, and now Todd was unloading them: bats, balls, helmets, and caps were beginning to make Todd's dream come alive. Every bat was an irresistible invitation to Todd to try it out with a ferocious 'air' swish and swing whilst Solomon watched and waited nearby. Everywhere that Todd went Solomon did too, but also, so did the red holdall, a fact not lost on the twins. They were sharp, nosy, and wanted to be in on everything.

'He's here again,' Mikey Junior moaned to his sister, 'I bet he knows what's in the bag.'

'It's just a bag with a water bottle,' Michaela responded with an air of calm, sensing her brother's jealousy.

Mikey Junior shrugged. 'He takes it everywhere. Even to the loo! It's weird!'

'Yeah, true!' Michaela agreed. 'And it's locked. I did see him with a wad of 'folding money' that I thought he put inside it.'

'Really?' Mikey Junior questioned, looking interested, 'lots of notes?'

Michaela nodded. 'I think so.'

'It 'ud be pointless asking him, though,' Mikey Junior gestured at Solomon, 'it's like talking to a brick wall. He never speaks.'

Solomon didn't need words, he spoke in pictures, pictures that he drew and gave to Todd, adding a few more to his growing collection after every visit. To Solomon, Todd was like an open book; his burdened past was transparent and the subject of many wonderful sketches. Every time Solomon gave him a picture from his time as a Rainbow Child, he acknowledged it as the 'Stig Man.'

'Only you know I'm the Stig Man, Dude,' Todd reminded him. It was a comfort to Todd that at least one person understood how he came to be there and, more importantly, that his staying was a deal with the Wobniar and only for as long as he could secretly and successfully sustain Angel Seraphina. She was his lifeline, and he was hers.

The twins watched as Todd handed Solomon a bat and gently pitched a ball for Solomon to hit. He missed it every time.

'I want a go!' Mikey Junior muttered, 'It's not fair!'

'Just ask!' Michaela said. She was the more sensible twin despite being the second-born and the youngest.

Before long, Todd was showing Mikey Junior how to bat, coaching the stance and swing whilst Solomon and

Michaela were learning to pitch. The pitchers struggled to deliver: they were either 'skying' the ball way too high, leaving it short, or hurling a grass cutter, skimming the ground so that Mikey Junior couldn't hit it. Todd knew that this practice mattered: one day, if his time had run out and Seraphina was in peril, he would need someone to pitch for him; he might need to score a vital life-saving home run to return to the Rainbow. Right now, the children were so in the zone of hanging out with Todd that they didn't see Tiggy cycle past in 'a dress to impress' date night outfit.

Tiggy's only contribution to the date was to show up. It was all down to her mother, from the man she was meeting to the outfit she was wearing. Seeing her daughter wearing a dress at the wedding had filled her mother's head with a new wardrobe of possibilities. The slip dress and choker she had chosen for Tiggy's date were not 'biker friendly' at all, nor were the pair of strappy high heels in a carrier bag hanging from her handlebars that would be the cherry on the cake once swapped out for her trainers.

Tiggy passed the Lightning Tree, happy to see that a few days on, the tent was gone, and Arthur was no longer guarding it; he handed over the baton to Alicia and her gang, who had devised a rota of camp-out shifts covering the council's hours of work. Besides, Alicia was confident that if push came to shove, a bribe or two would do the trick as in the past.

'You'd be surprised how many council bods in high places I've bought favours from over the years,' Alicia boasted. 'A tasty backhander with three zeros at the end will usually seal the deal.' There was no getting away from it: Alicia was fierce, shameless, and enjoyed her wealth and power.

❊ ❊ ❊ ❊ ❊ ❊ ❊ ❊ ❊ ❊ ❊ ❊

It had been a while since Tiggy had been on the dating scene. Gav was now officially an 'ex', and there was a void in her life that her mother was desperate to fill. Tiggy was just in the flow of trying to keep her mother happy, or rather, not so sad. Todd was not happy, though. His sinking feelings of annoyance and panic surprised him; the thought of losing out to someone else had stirred up emotions he had never had before. It had taken him a long time to find Tiggy, and whether she was 'the one' or not, he hoped to discover what was driving him to be with her. One thing was certain, though: Todd felt jealous.

However, Todd was not alone in feeling this way; the twins felt jealous, too, because Todd was giving Solomon a lift home in his 'cool campervan'.

'What's in there?' Mikey Junior asked as Todd put the holdall on Solomon's lap in the front of the van.

'Hop in the back, if you fancy a ride,' Todd said to deflect.

The twins didn't need to be asked twice, scrambling into the back, feeling like a king and queen. They drew the dinky curtains, putting their feet up on the long back seat, moving off Solomon's sketchbooks. Mikey Junior flicked through them, page upon page of brilliant drawings, too jealous to be impressed but pausing on a picture of Todd's holdall showing the combination lock's numbers, trying to memorise them.

'What's in the bag?' Mikey Junior whispered from behind into Solomon's ear.

'Leave him!' Michaela mumbled, 'You know he can't say.'

✳ ✳ ✳ ✳ ✳ ✳ ✳ ✳ ✳ ✳ ✳ ✳

Aqua Aura was the fanciest cocktail bar for miles, which partly explained the reason for the shift dress and choker. Underdressed and overdressed are a standard conundrum of a first date and can either help or hinder that crucial first impression; the chance of a second date can be won or lost right there. Tiggy had date night nerves and, choosing to be fashionably late, she expected to arrive last. She swivelled on her bar stool for twenty minutes without a sign of her mystery man. Tiggy didn't really care if it was a 'no show' but as she was there waiting, she sipped on a cocktail to settle her butterflies, unable to stop her head or her bar stool spinning whenever the door behind her opened.

Her glass was almost empty when a tall, dark, handsome stranger walked in. He was looking around for someone, someone he couldn't find.

Tiggy turned on her stool, staring over at the man, 'You'll do!' she murmured, her heart beating a little bit faster, hoping that this was him, her mystery date, all six feet of tan-skinned 'hunkiness'. However, the flutters did not last because the man soon spotted his girlfriend sitting with others at a far table, and that was that.

'Um, I thought it was too good to be true!' Tiggy muttered, taking a consolation final sip of her drink and was about to make a move for home when suddenly a man tapped her on her shoulder and thrust out his hand.

'Malcolm?' Tiggy asked, noticing his ankle swingers and bow tie as they locked hands. It was a feeble handshake like grasping hold of a limp lettuce.

'Call me Malc...as rhymes with talc,' he said, throwing back his pudding basin haircut and laughing as if he'd cracked the joke of the century.

There was a long silence, and Tiggy could feel her heart shrinking. It was going to be a testing evening, and her inner voice was already hailing a taxi.

'Can I get you a drink?' Tiggy asked when he hadn't offered to replace her empty glass.

Malc paused, 'Um, I should check with Mummy... Mother,' he corrected. He rolled up his trouser leg, removing a bamboo cylinder from his grey, ribbed knee-length sock, and stood it on the bar.

'Is that what I think it is?' Tiggy asked, looking horrified. It was a scatter tube of his mother's ashes.

'I still talk to Mother and run stuff by her; she knows whether my tablets don't mix well with alcohol,' he said. Malc placed his fingers on the top of the tube and waited. 'It's Mother's vibrations that guide me.' He paused again, 'p'raps best I stick to a soft drink? Who doesn't love a 7 Up!'

Tiggy was squirming, bewildered that her mother thought that this man could ever be a love match; Malcolm was giving a monotone and monotonous description of the tablets he took for what and when. The testosterone boost pills were not to be confused with his bladder control tablets that he always took after a meal.

'Will you be eating?' the bar man enquired.

Malcolm looked panicked. 'May I see the menu?' he said. 'So many things disagree with my sensitive tummy.'

Tiggy stared at the ground, wishing it would open and swallow her up. Malc was not the man she expected or hoped for, and when Malcolm excused himself for the 'Gents', Tiggy seized her chance to cut and run, leaving 'Mother' on the bar.

Todd would have laughed, being a fly on Aqua Aura's wall, watching the disastrous date, but as he pulled the van up outside Solomon's house, he thought another man was in town stealing Tiggy's heart. When Solomon got out, he stared with intensity at the twins still in the back, handing them a sheet of paper.

It was a sketch of a wingless angel in a flowing gown wearing a floral garland on her head.

Michaela giggled, 'Cute picture, but why the bridesmaid? We wanted to know what was in the bag!'

They didn't realise, but Solomon had told them everything. Whether it was telepathy or x-ray vision, Solomon could see exactly what was inside the bag: Angel Seraphina blinked her eyes and smiled, nourished by The Power of Two.

Chapter 17

GEORGINA'S POOR TIMING

Mikey Junior and Michaela loved their new home and the freedom to explore the woods and the surrounding farmland. BMX training filled most of their free time, and so they got up extra early every morning to visit ECM's therapy animals before school. They particularly loved the miniature donkeys 'Ned' and 'Nedder Again' and received the deep affection from these knee-high, chestnut brown friends that they 'nedder' got from their mother.

'I'm sure they know what I'm thinking,' Michaela said as Nedder Again pricked his magnificent ears and nuzzled against her. 'Todd says that about Solomon.'

'They do. They know everything,' Mikey Junior responded, rubbing Ned's white nose. 'Solomon knows nothing.' He couldn't hide his jealousy over the blossoming relationship that Solomon had with Todd.

Sundays were rest days for everyone but Mikey; the 'double time' shifts enabled him to buy stuff for the twins. For Tiggy, it was the morning after the night before, and she was describing her dating saga to Todd over a mid-morning breakfast coffee.

'He brought his mother with him!' Tiggy said grinning, 'His dead mother's ashes!'

'WHAT!' Todd exclaimed raising his eyebrows as his eyes bulged wide. 'Is this a joke?'

'I'm not kidding! It was a nightmare. 'Malc rhymes with talc' also has a sensitive tummy,' Tiggy said, giggling. She stared at Todd, so chilled and together and everything that Malc was not.

'Then I take it there'll be no second date?'

'There wasn't even a first date. I ran for the hills not long after 'mother' joined us. He's probs still sat there waiting!'

The two looked at each other and burst out laughing, unaware that the twins had returned and were hiding up, trying to listen. Todd fascinated them and they were completely under his spell, wanting to know everything about him.

'So, you're still on the singleton's market?' Todd enquired, locking eyes with her. Their gaze lingered, staying a bit too long to be normal. There was an obvious chemistry between them and Buddy, sensing the vibe, snuck down between them.

'Yeah, I'm a 'Lone Ranger' with the 'ex-factor.' I've got a string of them!'

Todd grinned. He liked everything about her: her quirks, style, and smile that made him feel a million dollars, as if the sun was always shining and the world was his.

'You crack me up!' he said, staring into her green eyes and getting lost in this Garden of Eden as he moved closer to her on the couch. He couldn't stop smiling at her.

Mikey Junior nudged his sister, 'D'ya reckon they fancy each other?' he whispered.

Tiggy couldn't help grinning back at him; there was an undeniable attraction, and as she fussed over Buddy snuggling up for her attention, she gave Todd a humorous rundown on her failed dating history.

The electricity was palpable, and sparks were flying enough to light up the Blackpool Tower. Timing is everything, and although it wasn't the right moment, Tiggy's sparkling green eyes were calling and spurring him on. His thigh was against hers, his heart was pounding, and his body tingled as he prepared to lean in and reveal his true feelings, but then...

'Only me!' called out Tiggy's mother, walking in and startling the young couple, not having heard her knock at the door.

They spontaneously pulled away from each other, trying to look casual as if nothing were going on. Georgina had no idea of her poor timing. Only Tiggy and Todd felt the turbulence like a storm in their hearts. What would have happened next? Did they both feel the same about each other?

'I was just on my way out, so I'll leave you ladies to it. It's good to see you, Georgina, and looking so well,' Todd said, grabbing his keys, baseball cap, and red holdall, smoothing his exit and hiding his embarrassment at the aborted 'first kiss.'

Georgina rubbed Buddy on his grey chin, completely oblivious. 'Well dear, how did it go? What did you think of Malcolm?'

'Malc rhymes with talc? Not a lot!' Tiggy said dismissively. Her mother's arrival was untimely, killing a moment with Todd that might not ever happen again. Her mother meant well but it sucked.

'Not bad boy enough?' Georgina suggested. 'Malcolm may not set pulses racing and he may not be what you want, but I reckon he's what you need.'

'Oh, please!' Tiggy responded with such disdain that her mother instantly deleted Malcolm from her mental list of potential sons-in-law.

'Todd seems lovely!' Georgina said, shifting her attention to another potential candidate. Tiggy shrugged her shoulders, her thoughts miles away.

As Todd arrived at the baseball field, his mind was spinning with the turmoil of the unanswered, knowing that he had revealed his hand. It was obvious where their couch session was heading, but what if Tiggy didn't like him in that way? She may even ask him to move out. 'Disaster' and 'idiot' were the words that kept buzzing in his head as he parked his campervan, loaded up with flat pack lockers for the new headquarters. It was nothing fancy: a small wooden outbuilding with space and a leak-proof roof, but it was a start.

Solomon was there as usual with his sketchpad and pens, waiting for Todd to arrive. Today his mother had dropped him off, Solomon making a heart with his thumbs and index fingers and waving for her to go. It was a Solomon-style 'I love you' and 'goodbye', 'I need my space'. It was always the same; simple and to the point, and was simply how he rolled. Solomon now spent so much time hanging out with Todd that Tanisha always knew where to find her son. In a strange way, the vibrant baseball-loving American was Solomon's happy place.

Outside of the home, the young savant was seldom far from Todd.

'Hey Dude! You wanna practise pitching today?'

Solomon nodded, passing Todd a sheet of paper that he had torn out of his sketchpad.

'That's cute!' Todd said, studying the picture of a romantic couple hand in hand, knowing it was he and Tiggy. Solomon's drawings always nailed the subject's likeness. Todd stared at his young friend. How did this kid know about the stuff he drew?

'Not sure about the holding hands, Dude. Sure, I dig her, but best we keep it just friends. We're housemates,' Todd said, looking wistful. 'Who knows how long I'm here?'

The sofa incident had thrown Todd's head into chaos, reminding him that he was there, but only by a conditional thread. Todd removed his holdall from the campervan, turned the combination lock's dial to release the zip, opening it for Solomon to see inside and for the sun's rays to flood in. Todd caressed the sunflower's petals and then pressed down on its brown centre until Angel Seraphina's face appeared.

'She needs me, and I need her. She is where my loyalties must lie,' Todd mumbled, just loud enough for Solomon to hear. 'She's the only reason I'm here.'

Solomon's photographic memory consumed every detail of the angelic face staring back at him, his thoughts only coming to life as he started to draw.

'She rescued me, Dude. Now I must keep her safe,' Todd said, staring at the sunflower and Seraphina's radiant smile. 'Like this,' he said, squeezing a few drops of rainwater from his water bottle onto her face for the sun to dry. Todd knew that Solomon would never say what he had seen, and the Vow of Secrecy was safe, and so, too, was Angel Seraphina. Her eyes were wide open. The Power of Two was at work.

Solomon began sketching again: images of Todd, as the Rainbow Child he once was. Todd glanced up at the brilliant blue sky.

'You don't ever want to know that place, Dude,' Todd said, getting glimpses of Solomon's drawing. 'I've tried everything to forget.' He stared into Seraphina's reassuring eyes that were like pools of melted chocolate and felt like a place of comfort. 'She sacrificed her wings to set me free.'

Todd was always relieved to see Seraphina's eyes gazing back at him, but anxious thoughts had moved in about his awkward situation with Tiggy. Whatever was he thinking? How could he throw it all away in one foolish, spontaneous moment?

Solomon worked his magic, his pens in free flow, body rocking with intensity of focus, drawing with fervour as Angel Seraphina, shielding Todd with her wings from the Indigo's deadly serpent, came to life on the page. As Todd stared at the powerful image, it brought a lump to his throat.

'I hope she knows how full of gratitude I am to her. I owe her everything,' he said before snapping himself out of his bubble and locking away the dark memories once more. 'C'mon Dude! Let's try that pitching action.' Todd plonked a baseball cap onto Solomon's head and handed him a ball.

Anything Todd suggested, Solomon was all in. He pitched the ball too high and sometimes too wide, but although not home run hitting contenders, he had greatly improved. Todd patiently put the boy's feet into position, repeatedly guiding his arm action; one day this practice might be vital for Todd to hit a life-saving home run.

Chapter 18

THE TESTING WEEK

The new week wasn't getting off to a good start. 'Monday madness' was already unfolding; Todd had lost his campervan keys and was late leaving for work whilst Mikey, just in from his night shift, was finishing off ironing the twins' school uniforms when an official looking envelope arrived that was about as welcome as a tray of pork pies at a bar mitzvah.

'Over my dead body!' grumbled Mikey, leaning over the ironing board reading a letter. This bombshell was the last thing he needed, battered and shattered after thirty-six hours without proper sleep. Mikey punched the board's surface in frustration.

'You OK?' Tiggy asked, breezing in from the kitchen, eating a piece of semi-cremated toast.

'The missus wants custody. She heard about the film and thinks they're gonna be 'Red carpet megastars'. She's counting and spending the dollars already!'

'They're short-listed. The Casting Director hasn't officially booked them yet.'

'She's so annoying!' Mikey muttered, not sounding like he meant it. 'Aaagh!' he yelled, bashing the board again.

The twins had slept in, skipping seeing the donkeys before school, and hearing their names mentioned, wandered through in their pyjamas, rubbing their eyes and taking their Game Boys off the table.

'I can't afford a fancy lawyer, but I know they're best off with me,' Mikey said, handing the twins their uniforms and lunch boxes.

'What's going on?' Mikey Junior asked whilst still concentrating on his Game Boy screen.

'Your mother wants you kids back, living with her.'

'Awh! But we want to stay with you, Dad,' Michaela said, nudging her brother for support.

'Yeah, I'm not going anywhere!' Mikey Junior agreed. 'We love being here with you, Dad.'

Mikey smiled, but he looked worried and defeated. 'It's always down to money! Money, money, money!' he yelled, thumping the ironing board once more.

All this time, Todd was turning the place upside down searching. 'Anyone seen the VW keys?' he asked, looking at the twins and trying to avoid eye contact with Tiggy after their 'near miss kiss' the day before. It felt so awkward.

'What about in your bag?' Michaela suggested picking it up. Todd snatched the holdall out of her hands, as Michaela looked a bit shocked. Usually, 'the king of cool' Michaela's play for the bag had agitated Todd, but then, finding his keys down the side of the sofa, his swagger returned.

The twins watched Todd from the window, talking to himself and setting his holdall on the campervan's passenger seat.

'Blimey, he's in a hurry!' Michaela said as the campervan throatily sped away. 'There's some't weird about him and that bag. Have you noticed? D'ya reckon he's hiding some't?'

'Dunno, but you're right. It's always with him...he behaves with it like we do with our Game Boys; it goes everywhere. He certainly never goes out without it,' Mikey Junior said, looking unusually deep in thought.

'D'ya think he's been on the rob and he's stashed the bag with cash? We don't really know him.'

'He doesn't look rich…'

'But why's he always checking on it, like it's precious?' Mikey Junior pondered, scratching his head.

'P'raps it's a secret, like he's hiding a gun or loads of Haribo,' Michaela suggested.

'Dunno, but I'm gonna find out.'

'We're gonna find out!' Michaela corrected. They fist bumped in silent agreement, having for the first time looked up from their screens.

❋ ❋ ❋ ❋ ❋ ❋ ❋ ❋ ❋ ❋ ❋ ❋

Tuesday was a clash of the former feuding Heavenly Gardens Titans: Alicia Gold and the Gotobeds. Unfortunately, for Tiggy, she ended up in the right place at the wrong time. She and Buddy had gone for a walk to the village's pet cemetery, where Starman Bowie, Buddy's father, was at rest, along with some of her own father's ashes. The annoying but harmless Emily Gotobed and her husband Paul were there, laying flowers on the graves of their poodles, Darling, and Princess. Tiggy knew she would face a tirade of questions: the couple had fled from the close, but their fascination for all things Alicia and Heavenly Gardens remained as strong as ever.

'So, what's Mrs Gold up to these days?' Emily asked with a sneer, holding Treasure, their fluff ball Pomeranian in her arms.

'Just being her usual annoying self,' Tiggy replied, resigning herself to a long interrogation.

'Not like that, you silly man!' Emily scolded, noticing her husband not shortening the stems of the lavish array of flowers he was arranging into a marble vase. 'You've scissors, man, use them!'

Tiggy wondered how, with Emily's fearsome tongue, Alicia had succeeded in driving them away.

'Isn't she trying to close you down?' Emily asked, trying to pacify Treasure, who had started to yap and wriggle. 'What is it, sweetheart?' she said, putting the dog down to have a sniff around in the longer grass. Emily Gotobed touched Tiggy on her arm, 'Don't let that woman bully you, dear!'

Her husband, for the first time, created the familiar ritualistic echo of old, 'Don't let that woman bully you, dear!'

'She's a brute!' Emily added, reinforcing her dislike of the woman.

'She's a brute!' Paul repeated, but sounding less nervous about his wife than when Heavenly Gardens was their home.

'I know. I won't,' Tiggy responded, thinking this couple had at least changed a bit for the better. Even Mrs Gotobed's shrill voice had softened.

'That woman made me a nervous wreck. Moving out of Heavenly Gardens was the best thing we've done.'

'The best thing we've done,' Paul Gotobed concurred.

Emily bent down, rearranging the flowers on the graves, her long-suffering husband still unable to get things quite to her liking.

Treasure, enjoying a rare off-lead opportunity, was exploring further afield when suddenly they heard Alicia Gold's distinctive rasping voice. The Gotobeds scurried for cover behind the nearest bushes, their peeping eyes glazed over with terror, not having come face to face with their adversary in years. Somehow, Treasure, as if she knew that the woman was an enemy, began chasing Alicia, yapping and snapping at her heels; the louder she shrieked, the more the four-legged fluff ball attacked. Tiggy scooped Treasure up in her arms, bracing herself for Alicia's wrath.

'Is that little beast yours?' Alicia shouted, glaring at Tiggy. 'It needs putting down! It gave me the fright of my life!'

Tiggy nodded as if the Pomeranian was hers, inwardly applauding it for having a go at 'The Bitch Queen'.

The Gotobeds, hiding in the bushes and hearing every word, hardly dared to breathe. Alicia was visiting

'Tiger', her tortoiseshell tabby cat. It had recently died from eating rat poison on its nightly, neighbourhood prowls, and Alicia wanted someone to blame. If she had known the Gotobeds, her favourite prey, were just metres away, she certainly would have gone in for the kill.

A reasonable start to Wednesday was later to turn pear-shaped. Rach, infatuated with Todd, often hung around at the baseball field on the off chance of seeing him, whilst Bo was at the track. After a rocky spell of nasty rows with her partner, Rach was a singleton once more and had designs on Todd being her next romantic understudy to her 'Take That' idols. By the time Rach picked her daughter up, she was grinning like somebody who had just won the lottery jackpot.

'Bo's had a cracking session, her starts were fire!' Tiggy said high-fiving Bo. Rach was thrilled, although not about her daughter.

'So that makes two of us. I've had a cracking session, too,' she boasted. 'I only gone and got me a date with the dishy baseball guy. Glad I binned off my fella! He was boring me right off.'

Tiggy's heart sank. She hadn't known how to handle the sticky situation with Todd, nor him, her, and the incident had caused an inevitable shift in their relationship, creating an awkward atmosphere at home.

'If you snooze you lose!' Tiggy mumbled under her breath, hearing Rach still boasting to anyone who would listen about her dating conquest with the 'campervan fit guy.'

It had been an odd week of unwanted surprises, but as Thursday dawned, yet more trouble was in store when another third party encroached upon Tiggy's world and caused drama: Jessie Jennings loved ECM's therapy animals more than she did humans, often spending time with them whenever her world felt broken. Snowdrop, the little white Falabella pony, was especially in tune with Jessie, always managing to calm and heal her. She didn't mind Jessie rocking and humming when she was anxious and it made her feel safe and secure without judgment.

Jessie was happy after a 'no tears day' at school and had spent her 'positive reinforcement money' on her favourite sweets. Jessie wanted Snowdrop to be happy, too, and arriving early at ECM for Music and Movement with Miss Penelope, she wandered over to the pony grazing on the nearby fenced-off meadow, and ignoring the 'Do Not Feed' sign, shared her tubes of Rolos with Snowdrop. It wasn't long before the chocolate sweets were all gone.

Later that evening, Snowdrop was in distress, biting at her side and kicking her belly.

'What's up with the white pony?' a dad on the pick-up from ECM asked Penelope and Adam, who were getting ready to close for the day.

'Snowdrop? She's been fine,' Penelope responded, the couple tailing him outside and finding some parents and children trying to comfort the agitated pony rolling onto her side.

'She's sweating a lot,' Adam said, staring at the foamy substance on her neck. 'What's she eaten?'

'Her usual feed,' Penelope replied, unaware that Jessie was hiding behind people and covering her ears.

'Is she going to die?' Daisy kept asking. Blessings looked scared, asking to go home to avoid seeing it.

A little lad called Nathan, who was 8 years old, sat cross-legged on the grass, lining up his collection of plastic dinosaurs with great precision. The dinosaurs went with him everywhere, always in the same dinosaur shoe bag except for the T. rex that had a special place in his pocket. 'Will Snowdrop die standing up or lying down?' he asked, swapping out the Diplodocus standing alongside the Brontosaurus and replacing it with the Dilophosaurus.

'I'll call the vet,' Adam said, unaware that Jessie was crying, burdened with the guilt of her sweet intentions turned sour.

Friday morning brought more concerning news: Snowdrop had confirmed colic and needed painkilling drugs. The hope was for her to make a full recovery, but Jessie didn't know that. She had heard talk of possible surgical intervention if the colic didn't ease. She always had a busy brain, thinking, but overthinking. She felt overwhelmed by emotions: sadness for Snowdrop's pain, fear that she may not get better, guilt for feeding the pony her sweets, anxiety that the truth would come out, the pressure of keeping the secret, anger for her foolishness, and confusion that sometimes the sweetest deeds could turn sour. Jessie didn't know what to do: it was either fight or flight, and Jessie's response was the latter.

Jessie never returned from school that day. By teatime, the search was on as her frantic family and many of the villagers combed the area looking for any signs of Jessie Jennings, aged 10, dressed in her red and white check school dress. She was young in her ways and very trusting, perceiving everyone as her friend. The police and their dogs were a reassuring yet alarming presence; imaginations were running riot amongst the search party, but one thing that everyone agreed was that they needed to find the vulnerable child quickly before trouble found her.

'She won't have gone far,' Penelope said trying to convince herself as she and Adam checked the premises of Every Child Matters. Jessie's red Wellington boots were standing by her coat hook, and her clay model of Snowdrop was still unfinished, awaiting its legs. There was no sign of Jessie. The newlyweds carried on searching outside, holding hands as they headed for the Lightning Tree. The evening sun cast a gloriously warm pink light over the tree's branches as the sun was sinking like a fireball onto the western horizon. It was potentially a breathtakingly romantic scene, but it went unnoticed. Penelope and Adam just wanted to find Jessie.

As nightfall came, there was still no sign of the girl and the hunt continued by searchlight and torches. Tiggy roamed their farmland with Buddy off lead, as she hoped he would find Jessie's trail, sniffing out scents, and every so often, stopping to mark his territory by cocking his hind leg.

It was the best of the community, with everyone pulling together with the shared goal of bringing Jessie safely home. However, Alicia, the usual leading light for community affairs, was noticeable by her absence. The mood was sombre and determined, and nobody wanted to go home. Where was Jessie Jennings?

Friday merged into Saturday the search having continued through the night, the inky blackness eventually lifting as the sun came up, casting a rosy hue across the morning sky. Many had failed to sleep and whilst weary, they still strode out with purpose, methodically scouring the area, beating back bushes with big sticks, wading through fields of long grasses and overgrown paths and ditches, and venturing into the woods, the graveyard and all the village landmarks and beyond. Jessie had everyone guessing and stressing. In fact, with many of the usual activities abandoned and cancelled, Saturday disappeared as quickly as Jessie.

Sunday arrived with still no trace of the missing girl. On Friday afternoon, she had skipped registration. Nobody recalled seeing Jessie on the playing field at lunch break, eating her sandwiches in her usual spot. She always sat alone on the same sawn-through tree trunk, known as 'Jessie's stump'. The timeline for her disappearance was incomplete, and her last movements, unknown. Her parents elevated the investigation, making a heart-rending appeal on the local television and radio stations for any information. 'Missing' posters of Jessie's last school photograph appeared through letterboxes, pinned on telegraph poles, notice boards and in windows around the village. Somebody must surely know something to help.

At such times, regardless of beliefs, the church is so often the place where a community comes together to share the burden and support one another. Great Snubington was no different, and at 11 a.m., the church was full, most of the village, including the Greygoyles, having made it. Todd, too, stood at the back of the church with his red holdall by his feet.

'Such a sorry affair,' Arthur Ramsbottom whispered to Tiggy as they joined the rest of her family sitting in a pew near the front. 'It makes me think about that night.'

'When Arnold went missing?' Tiggy whispered back.

Arthur nodded. 'I wouldn't wish it on anybody; those poor people!' Arthur said, staring at Jessie's family, puffy-eyed and passing around the tissues.

'All Things Bright and Beautiful' was Jessie's favourite hymn, everyone hoping that if they sang it loudly enough she would hear. She didn't, but the vicar's words brought comfort and hope as he asked for the child's safe return. Jessie's mother was resting her head on her husband's shoulder, praying for a miracle, when suddenly Alicia Gold and Jessie marched down the aisle to surprised gasps of elation.

'She was in my shed. Too scared to go home because of some sick pony or other,' Alicia blurted out.

Jessie's mother hugged her daughter, smothering her in kisses, 'Snowdrop is better, sweetheart. No more running away!'

Chapter 19

THE OUTING

Two weeks later, daily life within the village had found its groove again. Nathan's dad pulled up in an old-fashioned coach outside the village hall, and a large group of children and parent volunteers from ECM and BMX Mania clambered aboard for the eagerly awaited trip to the newly opened Legoland. For many weeks, it had been an entry on their calendars, the ECMers needing good notice to process the change to their usual routine. They loved Lego, and a building competition for groups of six had sparked Adam's interest for the ECMers to shine amongst their peers. They had some good constructors who could tackle any building challenge with the best of them, and now they were all aboard for the shiny dream prospect of Lego bricks galore.

A few parents were hanging around, eyes glued to their child on the coach, waiting to wave them off. Scotty was the last to arrive, holding up his fingers in a cross to his mother to ward off the 'vampire's' goodbye kiss. It would be social suicide at his age. He was eleven and cool, and he wanted it to stay that way.

Once aboard, Penelope and Tiggy called out the registers amidst the noisy and giddy anticipation for 'The trip of all trips' as trailed by MJ and Scotty ever since their parents had paid and returned the attendance slip. The duo plotted and schemed—what they would do on the coach and then at the place itself. Not much of it involved Lego.

It was like any typical school trip with the mad dash scramble for the back seat, the kids prone to travel sickness sitting at the front, and the coach driver having only just turned on the engine when the back seat's rowdy passengers started eating their packed lunch. Tiggy wished that Todd had shown up; he had volunteered weeks ago to help herd the children, but undoubtedly, things changed overnight after the recent 'near kiss' incident. Tiggy had looked forward to his company, but his absence in the circumstances was no surprise.

'Aw, Todd's not here,' MJ said, looking down the coach from the back seat. 'He promised we'd hang out together.'

'He never did! He only asked if you were going!' Micky corrected, turning around from the seat in front.

'Hey MJ! You might be on the bus, but ya sis' has just thrown ya under it mate!' Scotty joked.

The back seat crew erupted with laughter and jostled MJ, Sid and Corey, tickling him in the ribs until he was giggling so much that it hurt. They were there 'for the LOLs' and the back seat crew would not be a worthy back seat crew if they were not harbouring a secret.

'Have you got it?' MJ whispered.

Scotty nodded, 'That's why I was late. Just couldn't catch the little sod!' he said, unzipping his slightly gaping rucksack a bit more.

'Cool!' MJ said with a huge grin as he looked inside the bag.

Suddenly, a motor horn was honking and making a din. It was Todd speeding along in his campervan, flagging down the coach to wait and hastily parking up. Tiggy was smiling a thousand suns on the inside when Todd jumped aboard, his red holdall slung over his shoulder, looking 'the master of cool' and taking a bow to claps and cheers. Tiggy's heart was thumping, and she half hoped he would sit next to her. Things were awkward between them, but a long journey might sort it out.

'Another near miss!' he said, fixing his eyes on Tiggy and winking, but seeing Rach in the seat behind, he bypassed Tiggy and sat down next to her. Rach simpered whilst Tiggy felt crushed.

'Thanks for coming,' Rach whispered, giving him her Take That rucksack to put on the overhead shelf.

'I wouldn't have missed it for all the Lego in the world!' Todd replied loudly enough for Tiggy to hear.

'I hope the nutcase with the chainsaw fetish isn't on here,' Rach joked, looking down the coach at the block of ECM children already absorbed in their travel games. She was talking about Simon, who was quietly twisting the rows of his Rubik's cube as quickly as his fingers could move, changing the jumbled faces to solid blocks of colour. He had no idea about Rach's prejudice, even when she moved Bo and Izzy into seats further away from him.

'Keep an eye on that one! He's dangerous!' Rach said in a hushed voice to her daughter as the engine restarted. Bo and Izzy stared at each other, shrugging their shoulders,

'He looks harmless,' Bo whispered behind her hand.

'Yeah, looks like a boff! Shall we 'Sweet or sour?' and Bo nodded.

The girls waved out of the window at anyone they saw: the strangers were 'sweet' if they waved back, or 'sour' if they ignored them. The idea soon spread with The Swiss joining in. Jessie sitting opposite, choosing to be on her own, watched them without letting on what she was thinking.

Tiggy felt silly for the surge of happiness when Todd got on the coach, but she was not able to 'unsee' the cheeky wink or stop thinking about it. She decided that if 'Rach' with her weird boy band obsession really was his type, then she most certainly was not. They were like night and day, and now she had to endure their annoying chat, drifting over the top of her headrest from behind.

Over recent weeks, Penelope had been watching Tiggy and Todd closely.

'I think they like each other,' Penelope whispered to Adam.

He nodded, 'Yeah, watch this space!'

Penelope walked the coach, handing out the 'I'm Lost' name and contact number stickers for the ECMers to attach to their sweatshirts. Toby and Eli, 'the silent brothers,' who were 'in synch' without the need for words, were deconstructing Toby's model of Tower Bridge to build it again. Harry was behind them, mumbling the words to 'The Wheels on the Bus' like a machine on repeat, and Simon, sitting across the aisle, was still Rubik's cubing but with his eyes closed. Theo was next to him, staring at his travel chess set's reflection in the window as he visualised 'the perfect game', talking through his strategy without moving the pieces. Two seats along, Blessings was fiddling with Daisy's hair, trying to plait it like her 'My Little Pony's' mane, watched by Angelica, who was sitting opposite, grazing on her blueberries.

'Settle down!' Penelope instructed the rowdy backseat crew. She hadn't spotted Mikey Junior and Scotty executing number 3 on their planned 'Journey There Stuff to Do list'. The boys had filled empty crisp packets with water, and were lobbing them out of the small top window, but when Robbo made a direct drop of his tomato onto a car roof in the next lane, his crew went wild and even The Girls and The Lads conceded that it was a cool idea and joined in.

Omari, Leeroy, and Connor, sitting behind Nathan's dad, the coach's driver, were playing Dinosaur Top Trumps whilst Nathan matched them up with the dinosaurs in his impressive collection. Nathan's dad, like his son, was into collecting stuff, too, and for him, it was anything coach-related, in fact, so much so, he had bought the coach! Sophie and Grace, sitting opposite at the front, nursed their Polly Pockets and Tamagotchi on their laps, each clutching hold of their sick bags, willing the journey done, whilst other ECMers wore headphones to quell the sensory overload from the rowdy BMXers at the back half of the coach. Solomon was one such child. He stared at the world outside his window, squeezing his pliable, squidgy stress ball to while away the time.

A few rows from the front of the vehicle, Rach was in 'grief mode' for the boy band's break up, telling Todd about every Take That gig she'd ever been to and how her backstage pass had bought her a 'Meet and Greet' with the boys.

'Little Mark said I looked like 'trouble', Rach said, smirking and stroking Todd's leg.

'Trouble with a capital T,' Todd replied, his eyes burning into Rach's 'Take That' tattoo on her wrist, as her hand crept onto his knee. Rach bored Todd, and she told him off for yawning. Tiggy grinned. She was glad that he was bored. She found their chat both irritating and yet irresistible, so much so that the back of the coach's antics passed her by: MJ and Scotty were 'Moony Maestros' pressing their bare buttocks against the windows, making their mates laugh and cheer. They were the kings of the coach: in that moment, anonymous, carefree, and untouchable to the outside world. Leading a boisterous sing-along, after Corey had won the 'best burp' and Harry the 'loudest trump' (when he wasn't even trying) the coach finally arrived at the destination, Harry's 'Wheels on the Bus' having gone 'round and round' countless times.

Legoland was all sorts of magic made from plastic bricks that included the huge 'Welcome' sign. It instantly whipped the children into a frenzy pushing and shoving their way off the coach, excited to take in the spectacular views across the park.

'Should we visit Liz for a cuppa?' Scotty shouted after Adam told them about Windsor Castle, the Queen's much-loved residence that once overlooked the former safari park and had traded real-life hippo, giraffe, and other animals for plastic dinosaurs.

'Does the Queen mind not seeing the lions and tigers from her castle?' Daisy asked. 'I would.'

'Good question! I don't know Daisy,' Adam replied.

'I might send her a letter and ask her,' Daisy continued, dwelling more on things past than present.

Some of MJ's gang sniggered, 'Who cares!' Micky said, 'It's still a cool place.'

'The Girls' whispered and giggled just as they usually did to anything that Micky said. They had spent the trip passing secret notes to each other.

The model village of MiniLand was a gentle introduction to the park's attractions, the fabulous Big Ben clock tower chiming on the hour amongst Europe's finest landmarks. Tiggy's crew was becoming impatient; they craved action, desperate to explore and wanted to do everything, and now.

One coach party with two distinct mindsets, and so the group split up until lunch. The ECMers needed time to adjust to this new world with surprises around every corner. They had already lost Solomon, who hated crowds, when he had pointed to the Hill Train to swerve the sea of bodies surging into the park on foot. Todd had stepped in; it suited them both; Solomon liked Todd, but he would also be the perfect foil to shake off Rach, whose Take That trivia on the journey had worn Todd down until he chose to 'Take That' no longer. Besides, Todd was guarding his holdall, trying to avoid any tricky questions.

The view from the Hill Train was magnificent, sweeping across an expanse of lush grassland to Windsor Castle, which nestled on the distant horizon. Solomon stared blankly, his brain like a sensory sponge, absorbing the detail of the old-fashioned carousel and the speedy carts spinning around in the giant spider's lair without even so much as a flicker. He was an artistic architect, constructing and creating a memory board of angles and detail to become a masterpiece later.

Tiggy's gang had found Lego City. Rach, given the brush off by Todd, was now the tag-along helper joining forces with Robbo's mum, a ruddy-cheeked woman who drank too much, was down with the kids, and had a young sense of style.

'Cars made from Lego. This is mental!' Robbo shouted, taking the wheel of a brightly coloured electric car, lining up with MJ, Scotty, and 'The Lads' to race each other around the Lego City's roads.

Meanwhile, Penelope and Adams' group were taking a sedate boat ride through 'Fairy Tale Brook', home to lots of childhood favourites. The characters, all built from Lego with moving parts, seemed alive as they played out their story: Hansel and Gretel had found the house built from candy, the Three Little Pigs were huffing and puffing, whilst a prince was kissing Sleeping Beauty. Everyone was happy until the sight of the Billy Goats Gruff and the nasty troll lurking beneath the bridge frightened Jessie, and as their boat approached to pass beneath it, she closed her eyes, covered her ears, and curled up into a ball, pretending that none of it was really happening. Jessie kept in her foetal position, missing Little Red Riding Hood's meeting with the nasty wolf, and stayed that way for the rest of the ride.

'The Swiss' and 'The Girls' loved to grab the glory whenever they could, and were gloating over their Lego City souvenir driving licenses to anyone who didn't have one. The others had already moved on to the Boating School to navigate the meandering waterways in a fleet of brightly coloured battery-powered Lego boats. Scotty cut in on the inside channel, taking the racing line to overtake Robbo, but the two boats collided like dodgem cars. The racing instinct amongst the BMXers was bubbling over, Micky exploiting the skipper's error to overtake them both.

Solomon, meanwhile, had moved from one train to another, taking several laps of the park on the 'I Spy Express'. Onlookers waved, but Solomon never waved back. He didn't know them.

By lunchtime, when the coach party regrouped, the smiles were wide, and the clothes were wet.

'That elephant got me right in the ear!' Bo said, combing her wet hair, referring to the Lego elephant squirting water at the boats as they passed.

'Look how drenched I am!' Robbo boasted.

'Not compared with me, I'm the wettest.' Scotty claimed.

Micky sneered. Scotty annoyed her with how he always tried to outdo everyone.

'I let it spray me for ages. That's why I finished last,' he said.

'You got stuck more like!' Micky challenged.

Daisy disliked the bickering, 'Miss said it's not a race. There's no first and last.'

However, if the morning's activities weren't competitive, they were in the afternoon.

At three o'clock, it was the party's time slot for 'The Champion Constructors Competition'. It was an age-related challenge for teams of six to view and then build a previously unseen Lego model, points awarded for accuracy of colour, size, scale, formation of bricks, and the amount completed in the set time. Various groups had competed throughout the day for the title of 'Champion Constructors', each in their own booth to prevent copying or seeing other teams' progress. Toby and Eli sat outside ECM's, refusing to build anything other than Tower Bridge.

'What about our secret weapon?' MJ asked, nudging Scotty. 'Nerds are demons at Lego. We can't let ECM beat us!'

'I'm on it!' Scotty replied, bringing two cupped hands out of his rucksack as he struggled to hold onto a rodent that was wriggling and to conceal its long tail. By the time Scotty joined his team, he had already sneakily deposited the gerbil into ECM's booth.

The unseen build resembled a multi-storey car park, each level made of different coloured bricks. Simon had memorised it almost as soon as he looked at it, with seconds to spare, and when the 20-seconds viewing time was up and the klaxon sounded for the teams to start building, Team ECM was already organised into pairs of engineers, builders, and suppliers. In MJ and Scotty's booth, it was a different story; their competitive streak worked against them: six chiefs trying to lead and shout the loudest, the build was chaos. In contrast, at the midway stage, Team ECM had calmly completed four out of the seven storeys and in the correct colour sequence. Their build was progressing well when foul play intervened; Leeroy, who was busy sorting bricks into different coloured piles, spotted the gerbil, quitting his supplier role to hide beneath the table. It was a planned act of sabotage and an unplanned response: Sophie and Theo, deep in their builder's bubble, were undeterred, still building at pace while the gerbil scampered over, under, and amongst the bricks. Scotty's secret weapon to disrupt had failed as Simon, the remaining supplier, handed over the final bricks, before casually catching the little creature by its tail.

When the klaxon sounded for time up, Scotty, MJ, and Robbo had fallen out, Micky was in tears, Bo and Izzy weren't speaking, and their construction was an epic failure. Later, when the judges announced ECM the winners of that day's 'Best Build' competition, the team walked tall and proud back to their coach wearing their gold medals around their necks.

Chapter 20

LIFE IS UNFAIR

It was a new week, new term, and the day after 'the trip of all trips'. Penelope arrived at the farmhouse with Nureyev in time to catch everyone at breakfast. The twins, just back from their early morning visit to see the therapy animals, shovelled down their cereal, their clean school uniforms at their mercy. Mikey was singing 'Achy Breaky Heart' in the shower, and Todd, typically on his way out for work around this time, seemed to be hovering. He wanted to speak to Tiggy to clear the air, but then Penelope had turned up unannounced.

After the trip, Nathan had discovered that one of his precious dinosaurs was missing. Every night Nathan and

187

his mother went through the same bedtime routine: she drew her son's curtains, sprayed his pillow with 'sleep mist', put his Dino slippers by his desk, pointing towards the door, and sat his plush Dilophosaurus on the right side of his pillow close to the matching dinosaur on his wallpaper. Nathan had his own routine: lining up his dinosaurs in alphabetical order on his windowsill and drinking his bedtime hot chocolate, always from the same Jurassic Park mug. The process never changed, keeping Nathan calm, and settled and more likely to sleep. The discovery of the missing dinosaur had sparked an emotional and tearful meltdown. His dinosaur line up had a glaring gap between his Raptor and Triceratops: where was Stegosaurus? A frantic search ensued, but the conclusion was that the dinosaur had been 'lost in action' in the park.

'Has anyone found a Stegosaurus by any chance?' Penelope asked, explaining how much the dinosaur mattered to Nathan and the spin-off consequences for his family. The twins carried on eating, Mikey Junior spluttering out some Shreddies as Michaela kicked him under the table. Mikey Junior was a bad loser and had taken the dinosaur as revenge for their team losing in the construction competition. Tiggy shook her head. Michaela kicked Mikey Junior again, this time a little harder. Her brother gave her a death glare that nobody else noticed.

'Get a shift on!' he instructed, watching his sister gulp down her last spoonfuls of cereal.

Mikey Junior and his slightly guilty conscience were out of the door in a flash, Michaela grabbing her book bag and lunchbox, running to catch up.

Todd looked at the sisters sitting in cosy chat with Buddy and Nureyev slumped down together, and having missed his opportunity, he picked up his holdall and left them to it.

Tiggy sighed all the way down to her trainers. Penelope knew her sister inside out.

'You like him, don't you!' Penelope asserted, 'Be honest!'

Tiggy was under his spell, but she didn't wish to admit it, 'Maybe a little...'

'If you like him, tell him! What would a Spice Girl do?' Penelope asked.

'He likes Rach,' Tiggy responded.

'He likes you more!'

'He's got a date with her.'

Later that day, Tiggy was at the track before training. Today, she would be selecting the junior squad members for the UK Championships. She always dreaded seeing the faces of those who hadn't made it. She had dangled the carrot for months so that they would turn up and work hard. It was brutal: only two girls and two boys from each age band would be eligible. She looked through the feedback notes, competition results, and times. It was never easy playing God with their dreams.

'Don't look so serious. It might never happen!'

Tiggy looked up and saw Todd staring at her. His holdall, as usual, was by his side, his 'can't be without companion' like she hoped to be.

'I thought I'd just swing by to ask a favour,' Todd said, sounding unusually nervous.

'And…?' Tiggy asked.

'It's about Rach. She comes here, right?'

'She drops off and picks up,' Tiggy responded, not sure which way the conversation was heading.

'So, you don't really see her, not to speak to?'

'Kinda,' Tiggy said, not being the usual 'eager beaver' to be helpful and Todd knew it. 'Forget I said anything,' he said, starting to walk away.

She wouldn't let him go, not without answers.

'I could see her the day after tomorrow if you wanted me to.'

Todd hesitated. 'Seriously?' Todd's eyes were penetrating Tiggy's. There was a spark of something more between them.

Tiggy nodded, 'Sure. What's up?'

'It's my date with Rach she told me I'm going on. I've tried to bail but she's making it awkward and says she's bought tickets.' Todd scraped the ground with his baseball boot, embarrassed about his predicament with the 'Take That' super fan who blatantly wasn't his type either 'on paper' or anyhow else.

Tiggy's heart was warm like a hug from the inside out, 'So where do I come in?'

'I thought you could somehow tell her that we're together...' Todd said, gauging her reaction.

'Us, an item? Like an official couple? Even after yesterday on the coach?' Their eyes locked together; Tiggy and Todd burst out laughing at the absurdity of the situation they were trying to rescue. 'So am I to 'Take That,' you're not interested in 'Raunchy Rach!' Excuse the pun!'

They laughed, their eyes shining, both feeling the electricity pulsing through their veins.

'Sure! I'll think of something to get you off the hook. Consider it done!'

In that moment, they both knew it was just a matter of time before the near-kiss sofa scenario played out again. It wasn't a case of if, but when.

Back at the farmhouse, Mikey had opened his post. Sapphire wanted a divorce and custody of the twins, and she had hired a top solicitor for the purpose. Her legal proceedings were gathering speed, and with a date for a hearing in a few weeks' time, 'See you in court' was the message. Life wasn't fair. Sapphire was the 'wrongdoer', the one who had cheated, and yet now, on a whim, the twins were going to make money and a 'Red Carpet', she thought she should have them back. Mikey gave the twins his heart; Sapphire gave them nothing.

Todd was also on the wrong side of life's fairness counter; although he was free, he was also in chains: Angel Seraphina depended on his constant nurture and The Power of Two. It was a lot, and the need for secrecy was such a burden. At the end of each day when his weary eyes wanted to close, what mattered was that Seraphina's eyes were open. Todd had gone to the baseball ground to prepare for his grand opening, spits and spots of rain having started to fall. He removed the sunflower halo from his holdall, holding it in the sunlight, allowing the rain to do its job. Some days like today, saving Seraphina was easy; as raindrops fell onto the sunflower's rich raw umber centre, he watched his angel's face appear as it always did. Eyes open, she looked at peace, soaking up the sun's goodness until she had had her full replenishment and faded away, a blurred beauty of satisfaction until tomorrow.

Later that day, the life is so unfair vibe continued, spilling onto the track as Tiggy announced 'the chosen ones' for the UK Championships.

MJ had fist pumped the air, uttering 'Get in!' and Micky had spun around on the spot with a 'yes girl!'

when Tiggy called out their names. No surprises there, the twins were hungry for success with a daring flair and elite skills. On their day, they would win the race at the gate and be unstoppable. Suki claimed another place as the best of the rest of the girls. However, the shock inclusion was Robbo. He had hit a purple patch of form that had impressed Tiggy, but Scotty wasn't having it. There was nothing gracious about Scotty.

'It's a stitch up!' he grumbled, throwing his helmet onto the ground. 'His ol' lady has been creeping and sucking up for weeks. Even came on the trip! It's just so unfair!' Scotty stormed off muttering that it was his punishment for the trip's antics with his sister's gerbil.

When the twins arrived back at the farmhouse buzzing with their good news, Mikey was drowning his sorrows with cheap cider.

'How is this fair?' Mikey questioned. 'I want you here with me. You want that too, but your mother, 'cos of her fancy lawyer, will win.'

'Awh, that's horrid!' Michaela said, squeezing her father's hand. 'Her new fella hates us. They care about themselves and the baby, and that's it!'

'Yeah!' Mikey Junior pitched in. 'We're just Bobbi's babysitters.'

'I'm gonna fight for us,' Mikey said. 'Her bloke may be wadded, and I might not have a fancy lawyer, but I do have this,' he said, touching his heart, 'and when I lose, which I will, we'll at least know I've tried.' Mikey kissed the tops of their heads. 'I'm your dad, and nothing will ever change that.'

The twins hugged him so hard, not wanting to let go.

'If only you could have a fancy lawyer, too, we'd defo win,' Michaela said, still holding onto the hug.

'Life's just so unfair!' the twins said simultaneously, looking into each other's desperate eyes for answers.

Chapter 21

PANNA COTTA OR BLANCMANGE?

'It has to be money,' Mikey Junior concluded. 'Why else is it glued to him?'

Michaela shrugged. 'Dunno. Even if the bag is full of cash, we can't steal it. Not off Todd.'

'Dad needs it for a lawyer. Do you want us to have to go back to Mum's? You hate her posh bloke as much as I do.' Mikey Junior was trying to justify stealing the bag.

'I get it and sure I want to stay with Dad and yes, Mum's fella is stuck up, but we still can't take money from Todd...can we?' Michaela looked anxious, but half wanted her brother to persuade her.

'We wouldn't be stealing, just borrowing. When we're film stars, we'll be rich and pay it all back. I promise!'

It was true that the casting directors were close to confirming the twins for the hyped blockbuster feature film, starring an Oscar-winning actor and a handsome payout.

'But what if...' Michaela began.

'Not what ifs,' Mikey Junior interrupted, 'if we don't get money from somewhere, Dad's gonna lose in court. He told us that.'

Michaela reluctantly nodded, knowing that when her brother got something into his head, he would do it anyway. The idea of finding out what was in the bag seemed fun when she had thought it could be full of sweets, but now it was different. Her brother was serious about their father needing the money.

'Well, at least give Nathan his dinosaur back,' Michaela said, trying to lessen her guilt.

'Nathan can have his stupid dinosaur back!' Mikey Junior conceded. 'Are you gonna help get the bag?'

They fist bumped in silent agreement. All they needed to do now was to decide the time, the place and the how.

Mikey Junior fumbled in his 'Stuff that doesn't go anywhere else' tin and produced the missing Stegosaurus.

'I guess we'd better return it so cry-baby Nathan can sleep tonight!' he said in a mocking tone. 'I'll sneak it back so it looks like it was there all the time.'

'Don't be so mean. It wasn't Nathan's fault they won. They were better than us,' Michaela mumbled as they headed out of the house.

Every Child Matters was a hive of activity: spirits were high since the team's Lego building competition success. When the twins arrived to return the dinosaur, a boy called Stu and his mother were getting the ECM tour. According to the woman, 'Stu' was 'definitely normal' but, having heard about 'the trip of all trips,' he had become fixated with the place.

'We have something here for everyone,' Penelope said, taking the visitors into the pottery room housing a potter's wheel, a kiln and lots of pots in varying degrees of wonkiness, waiting to be painted and glazed.

'I'm just worried that if Stu starts coming here, as much as he might enjoy it, he will then get labelled,' the boy's mother said, concern written all over her face.

'Labelled?' Penelope questioned, 'I presume you don't mean Heinz 57 varieties or Prada and the like?'

The woman stared, stuck for words, 'Stu's normal, that's what I mean.'

Adam, hovering just outside with Theo, overheard and frowned.

'She's thinking what it suits her to think,' Adam mumbled. He knew it often happened.

'But have you cured any of the children that come here?' the mother asked. Adam stepped in.

'Fortunately, there is nothing to cure,' he said politely. 'I first opened this social space for my brother,' he said, gesturing to Theo, 'to feel connected to the wider world. Our ethos is in the name because we truly believe that, 'Every child matters.' Who doesn't want to feel like they belong and can be themselves? We try to do just that. We're not a school and some of the children travel miles to come here, for this safe space to explore what they like and find themselves.' Adam looked at the woman's unresponsive face. 'Many of the children feel lost outside of their home. Here, they don't need to mask because they feel accepted. We don't force square pegs into round holes.'

The woman shrugged her shoulders. 'I know some of the kids who come here. They're ...' she hesitated, searching for the 'right' words, 'they're different.'

'Yes, they are,' Adam said, forcing a smile, 'Please allow me to show you some of the ways that they're different, if Stu would like to?'

Stu was about 8 years old and as big as Theo, who had recently turned 11, accepting the invitation with much more enthusiasm than on his mother's face.

The boys looked like equals as they toured the various rooms and displays until they entered 'The Scientist's Space Lab.' Theo suddenly entered another dimension.

This was his world, and his knowledge elevated him to the stature of a giant. Theo smiled as soon as he saw his own mechanical model of the solar system and needed no prompting.

'The orrery, some call it a planetarium, is the Copernican system,' Theo said, pointing at his model. 'The sun is placed at its centre.'

Stu's mother raised her eyebrows, unsure what to think, but Stu was fascinated. His eyes followed the model's planets moving around the Sun and the Moon and orbiting the Earth at the right relative speeds.

'Theo has spent countless hours building it. The model is precise,' Adam said proudly.

Theo was showing Stu each planet, stopping in front of Saturn.

'These rings should be ice with dust and rock particles,' Theo said, looking at Saturn rather than Stu.

'There are lots of creative and critical thinkers here. We support their 'outside the box' ideas,' Adam said, watching how much Theo and his model continued to fascinate Stu. 'Is there anything you'd like to ask us?'

'Would I have to have a label to come?' Stu asked, remembering his mother and Penelope's earlier conversation.

Penelope smiled, 'No label needed. You're fine, Stu, just as you are!'

'I guess Stu being happy should be factored into it,' his mother conceded. 'He might at last find something he's good at!'

Penelope and Adam's eyes met, realising that this mother's sharp edges may take some softening before she fully got it.

'Why have panna cotta children to blend them into bland blancmange? That's what I always say,' Penelope concluded.

'Please, can I start?' asked Stu, looking hopefully at his mother.

'We'll have a think about it,' Stu's mum replied, hurrying him out of the door in case someone saw them there.

Outside, Alicia and her mob were marching with placards, continuing the protest opposing the local Council's new road and housing development proposals.

'Save our trees, save our track, because Every Child Matters,' they chanted.

Stu's mum stared at the placards, 'but what's wrong with blancmange?' she mumbled.

Chapter 22

THE CAMPERVAN TRIP

The twins were browsing the recently updated club notice boards that Tiggy refreshed every week with BMX Mania news items, training stats and competition results. A newly pinned bright orange flyer caught their eye.

'It's Todd's Open Day,' Michaela said, reading it aloud.

'Hallelujah!' Mikey Junior responded, not knowing what it meant. Robbo's Mum said it at her boy's selection for the UK Championships, and he had thought it sounded cool.

'He's been a right fuss pot getting everything just so,' Michaela mumbled, 'thought it 'ud never happen!'

The cogs were turning in Mikey Junior's head. 'Loads of people, lots going on, Todd distracted, it's the perfect time to take his holdall.'

'Um yeah, but must we?' Michaela asked, scanning the rest of the notice boards and checking out her feedback.

'We've no choice if we don't want the courts sending us back to Mum's and her ghastly bloke.'

'They were talking about moving to Portsmouth,' Michaela added.

'Then we'd be stuffed! It'ud be bye-bye to this place and Dad.'

'Yeah, it sucks!'

Mikey Junior looked at the flyer's date, 'Two weekends before the UK's. It'll be pips!'

'We're only borrowing it,' Michaela reminded him.

Her brother nodded, 'Partners in crime!'

'Partners in Crime,' she echoed, fist bumping to their alliance.

Todd had worked hard in his free time to get everything right and ready for his Open Day. Great Snubington was about to become the destination for all things baseball, the focus for the Brits to fall in love with the sport. He was spreading the word, heavily advertising the event, and his campervan had taken him everywhere, posting flyers on all the village notice boards, in windows, and even on the telegraph pole near the bus stop. Todd had cast his net further, too, advertising in the nearest towns and villages. The only thing still outstanding on Todd's 'to-do' list awaiting its tick was a trip to the city with a van full of flyers and posters and a visit to the local radio station for a live interview.

'Fancy it?' Todd asked Tiggy. 'It sure would be cool to have you on board tomorrow.'

Tiggy felt a surge of excitement. Todd was asking for her company, alone time, just the two of them. That never happened at home with Mikey working unsociable hours and the twins always around wanting a slice of Todd. He never minded hanging out with them, but it made him in demand. Todd's blue eyes were piercing, staring at her, wanting an answer.

Tiggy paused as if she was consulting her diary, 'Yeah, go on then!' she eventually replied. She was excited and, apart from her track commitments, she would have dropped anything to go, but the little voice in her head was telling her to 'play it cool' and not to 'do a Rach on him.'

The next morning, the housemates set off together for the radio station. Tiggy had never been in Todd's campervan, and she wondered how many females had sat in the passenger seat before. According to Todd, the answer was 'not many' and usually it was his holdall, 'his special lady' as he put it, but today, his bag was in the back.

They passed Alicia near the school, collecting signatures on a petition opposing the proposed development. As much as Tiggy disliked her, she admired her tenacity.

'I think the woman is growing on me a little,' Tiggy remarked, looking out of the window at a queue of people lining up to sign it.

She was enjoying the ride in the campervan with its cute curtains and cool driving companion, especially the easy, free-flowing chat punctuated with humorous banter.

'So, you always wear odd socks?' Tiggy said, querying Todd's confession.

'Sure! Who has the time to match socks? Besides, it sorts out your left and your right.'

'So, that's what put the 'odd' into Todd!' Tiggy joked, 'I once knew someone who could tell the day of the week from how he wore his boxers.' She was referring to her Rainbow Child experience when the Stig Man, trapped in the rainbow wore his underpants in various ways to keep check of the days. Todd didn't flicker, still hiding his identity. 'Kinda had you down for the 'commando' type of guy? Too busy being Action Man to wash your smalls!'

Todd laughed, the conversation getting flirtier.

'That's for me to know and you to find out!' Todd said, grinning.

Tiggy giggled, their eyes meeting. They both knew that their feelings were the same, tingling with anticipation as Todd pulled up in the Radio Station's car park.

'Stick it in neutral, would ya please!' Todd asked with a little smile.

Tiggy put her right hand onto the gearstick, Todd placed his left hand on top, locking it in, and turning to kiss her. Finally, after a month of trying to avoid one another and denying their feelings, the time felt right to seal the deal. There could never be another 'first kiss' but they both hoped that it wouldn't be the last.

However, if romance was blooming for Todd and Tiggy, Mikey was at war with Sapphire. The divorce papers had hit Mikey hard, just seeing it officially in black and white that the legal proceedings from his childhood sweetheart were in motion. Mikey had never thought it would happen, and it was difficult for him to accept that it really was over. He had wrestled with his misplaced feelings for months, and every time he was starting to heal, something would occur, like a chance meeting to re-open the wound. Today was one such occasion: Mikey was birthday shopping for the twins when he unexpectedly bumped into Sapphire. She looked right through him with winter in her heart; it was hard to believe that they had ever been close.

'How can you afford those when you're so skint?' Sapphire asked looking at the trendy trainers Mikey was buying.

'Never heard of overtime? I'll do whatever it takes,' he replied.

Sapphire sneered, 'You're trying to bribe them with stuff you can't afford.'

'It's not your business anymore what I do or spend my money on.'

Sapphire stared at him in his tired-looking clothes with contempt, 'As if I care! You're a loser in life and in court.'

'Just do one!' Mikey snapped, turning his back on his first and last love. He still thought Sapphire looked beautiful, just not now on the inside anymore, but the chance meeting would set him back and once again make her his first and last thought of the days ahead.

Later that evening, when Tiggy was back at the track drilling her 'comp' squad for the pressures and rigours of the 'UK's,' as they referred to the national championships, she felt different inside. A deep happiness underpinned everything she did. It was the power of the kiss, the power of Todd.

Chapter 23

THE OPEN DAY

The days leading up to the baseball Open Day flew by with Tiggy and Todd stealing a few precious moments: little looks across the breakfast table, secret kisses in the farmhouse's walk-in pantry, and private jokes about Todd's odd socks and how he may now have found his perfect match. They had even spent time together away from the house in the campervan, drawing the curtains and shutting out the world. For now, things were unofficial until after the Open Day and the UK Championships, not to distract from the task ahead and allow the giddy feelings to rule.

The Open Day came first, and at 10.30 a.m. on Sunday, 27th April, the bunting was up, and a well-drilled troupe of cheerleaders were frothing up a match day vibe to greet the first trickle of interested wannabe baseball players. Todd had created the 'all American dream': sizzling hot dogs, pretzels, peanuts, ice cream Klondike bars, and Cherry Coke 'slushies'; the kids, once there, would want to stay, either getting involved in the play or snack their way through the day, enjoying a flavour of American culture and the live action energy of a typical ballpark. The twins were amongst the first to arrive and were initially so excited by the atmosphere and entertainment that they had forgotten the real reason that they were there—Todd's holdall. The place was buzzing: the locals had turned out, whilst many others had travelled a distance to enjoy the unseen before event. It was the biggest thing to have happened in the area for a good while. Todd had pulled off a marketing triumph.

By early afternoon, the Open Day's lively atmosphere was at fever pitch: a large crowd had gathered to watch two guest teams from the London Mets playing in a 'friendly' match. Arthur Ramsbottom was in a prime spot for comfortable viewing, and sitting on his fold-up camping chair, he had dozed off in the sun until an excited, noisy crocodile of children, led by Penelope and Adam, woke him on their way to ECM's designated section of seats away from the crowds. Nathan had brought his dinosaurs and Simon his Rubik's cube, whilst Theo had his own baseball that he was gently throwing and catching. To Theo, baseball was a science, and he was excited to watch the various ways the pitchers made the ball move. Nureyev slumped down beside them, a willing object to stroke for comfort if needed. There was a high turnout from the local schools, and of course, The Girls, The Lads, and The Swiss were there. Nobody had wanted to miss it, and even those with zero interest in sports had showed up, driven by their FOMO, knowing that the event would be the talk of the village for many days, weeks, and months.

Todd was in the groove, his red holdall never far away and guarded by Solomon, his silent shadow. He was ramping up the energy and engaging the audience by triggering a Mexican wave around the ballpark seating. Adults and children alike joined in, loving being a part of what felt more like a show than a sporting event. The organ music played as the first batter strode out to the home plate. This was it: Todd's baseball dream coming to life.

'I want to see a curveball,' Theo said as the pitcher took the ball. 'It's the Magnus Effect that does it and the difference in relative airspeed at different points on the rotating ball's surface.'

'Is that so?' Adam said, smiling at Theo's enthusiasm for the physics of the sport. Every day, Theo taught him something new.

'Aw!' Theo sighed, after the ball pitched, 'straight and hard, resisting the pull of gravity a bit longer. Not a bend in sight!' he complained, 'and the batter didn't even hit it!'

'Let's hope someone can pitch one or he's not gonna be happy!' Adam whispered to Penelope, amused by his brother.

Rach, meanwhile, was milling around, wearing a 'Take That' baseball cap, keeping an eye out for Todd, not a bit interested in the ballpark play but only in his state of play with Tiggy. She spotted her rival at a food stall, feeding Buddy a sausage, and was happy not to see them together. The place was buzzing; however, not everybody was enjoying the razzamatazz: long-faced Greygoyles who usually would have opposed the new baseball club were now there in support, prompted by the village's change of circumstances.

'It's like rounders but vulgar!' Gertie Grimshaw griped from her wheelchair as the crowd went wild for the first home run.

'You could say it's 'base!'' said her husband, laughing at his little joke.

'Why would you when there's cricket?' she continued, missing his attempt at humour. 'But then of course, it's a gentleman's game and I don't see many of those here!'

'Agreed! Most of them are Americans from the base,' Timothy Grimshaw said, pointing to the pitcher and a few of the fielders.

'Deary me! It's like wartime Britain all over again,' muttered his wife, 'lock up your daughters!'

The starchy woman continued her commentary throughout the first few innings, interested only in the behaviour and not the actual play.

All this time, the twins were watching the match whilst keeping an eye on Todd and the bag.

'I can't believe Todd isn't playing, it's like he'd rather be with him,' Mikey Junior said, looking at Solomon contentedly drawing in his sketchpad and grazing on pretzels.

Tanisha was never far away, but the bond between Todd and her son gave her a breather to get the old Tanisha back for the afternoon to mingle. For a few hours, she was Tanisha, the bright and engaging woman with the big smile and afro, and not solely 'Solomon's Mum.' Todd was a blessing to them both, but it irked the twins.

'I wish I could make him disappear!' Mikey Junior said, scowling at Solomon. 'He's such a numpty! Why him? How is he so special?'

'It's certainly not his chat!' Michaela said with a giggle as they fist bumped it out.

As play continued with batters scoring as well as getting out, the twins knew that the clock was running down. When it became time for the 7th inning stretch, Todd signalled for the playing of the traditional anthem 'Take Me Out to the Ball Game', encouraging everyone to stand and sing the words displayed on a huge screen. Unexpectedly, Todd stepped onto the field to play. Mikey Junior nudged his sister, knowing it was their time to strike. Solomon was such an easy target; they could snatch the bag, and he wouldn't and couldn't say a word. It would be like taking candy from a baby.

Alicia Gold, having turned up late, was making her presence felt, leading the protest to thwart the new road, and housing development. She marched with her placard onto the pitch during play to catch some press attention. She never failed, and when she sat down in the batter's box, refusing to move, Alicia stopped play until two patrolling police officers carried her away. Alicia had made the headlines once more as the photographers got their scoop.

The commotion was the perfect distraction for the twins as everyone, including Solomon, stood watching Alicia in action. The twins seized the moment and the holdall too, slipping away with Mikey Junior's hoodie draped over it. It was so easy and, having escaped all eyes, confident nobody had seen, they fist bumped to their success. The holdall that had been like a part of Todd ever since they first met was finally theirs.

Back at the event, the London Mets B team had scored a victory over the A team, and the ballpark was now open for all to give batting and pitching a go. The children queued, waiting their turn for a player to coach them, whilst men channelling their inner Joe DiMaggio were straight into swishing the bat and trying to pitch the perfect curveball. Not so many women were having a go, although Rach, since her partner split and her more recent binning off from Todd was now on the hunt for a new man, and craving some male attention, tried to both bat and pitch. She loved the baseball players 'strong arms and firm grip' and made sure that everyone knew it: she wanted to make Todd jealous.

The event closed with the announcement of the winner of the 'Who are we?' competition: the public's opportunity to make their mark on the village and the club by giving it a name chosen by Todd. Over recent weeks, the entries had flooded in for the chance of winning a free year's membership, a baseball cap, and shirt. The 'Home Runners' popped up a few times, and 'The Curveball', too, was a popular suggestion in the mix, but 'The Snubington Slayers' proposed by an eminent Council Planning Officer's son was a front runner. The woman had some influence and could help them if the Club should remain on the threatened site. However, logic and strategy aside, another name jumped out, sucking Todd in to choose it: 'The Angels' proposed by Daisy Dingles. It surely had to be a good omen, but only Todd and Solomon knew why and how one special Angel was as precious to Todd as life itself.

Chapter 24

THE THEFT

The stallholders were clearing away, and everyone was heading for home. Todd's Open Day had been a triumph, and 'The Angels' were born. However, there would be no basking in glory or post-event celebrations: Todd had discovered that 'his special lady' was missing and nobody had seen anything, either actual or suspicious, to lead him to his holdall.

Surely, somebody must know something; Todd had trusted Solomon to keep his bag safe, but it was his own fault for assuming, and Solomon must never feel that he was to blame.

'You didn't see anything, did ya buddy?' Todd asked, checking Solomon's drawings from the day's events, but there were no clues.

Solomon was rocking and shaking his head, looking worried. He wanted to help if he could.

'Is it that important?' Tiggy asked as she helped Todd to search.

Todd ignored her; it was such a stupid question, but she meant nothing by it. How could Tiggy know about what was inside, and the jeopardy from losing it? Tiggy did not even know who he really was, and only Solomon knew about 'The Power of Two'.

By dusk, Todd was frantic, but thankful he had nourished Angel Seraphina before breakfast. The following days would be a different story if he didn't find her, and even worse if somebody else did. Not only would Seraphina be at risk, but 'finders, keepers' would be, too.

'I'm gonna check the trash again,' Todd said, but knowing deep down that it was pointless.

Tiggy nodded, 'Maybe someone's picked up the wrong bag by accident?'

However, the holdall was not the only thing missing because the twins were, too. Mikey Junior and Michaela, having perfectly executed the bag snatch, suddenly didn't know what to do with it. Everything about the holdall felt dirty: it was theft, and it belonged to their friend Todd, but they needed somewhere to hide it and keep the cash. Mikey Junior had already rationalised the whole episode as 'something that someone had to do'. In his mind, his parents' feud and his dad's desperation needed a hero, and he fitted the shoes.

Ned and Nedder Again were napping in the stable corner when the twins entered. The children flopped down into the hay, happy with their getaway and bumped fists, as they recounted how Solomon hadn't noticed.

'He's so dumb!' Mikey Junior concluded. 'It's his fault that Todd lost his bag.'

'So whatcha gonna do with it?' Michaela asked, but wondered why he had it in so much for Solomon.

Mikey Junior shrugged. He placed the holdall onto a hay bale like a prize exhibit in a gallery, climbing up a nearby stack and staring at it from the top bale.

'Open it, I guess,' he said, jumping down and waking the donkeys.

Ned and Nedder Again knew the twins well. It was usually early morning when they visited, but the donkeys loved their attention at any time of the day or night.

The twins just sat staring at the bag. 'What if it's not money inside?' Michaela asked. 'Then we'll have done all this for nothing, and worst of all, Todd'll know we're thieves. Tigs will kick us out, Dad included. Nobody likes a thief.'

'Nah! It's money. You saw Todd put wads of cash in there. We're only borrowing it, remember!'

'Don't blame me!' Michaela said, looking sheepish, 'I only said I thought I saw him.'

Mikey Junior shrugged. 'What's done is done and we've got it now.'

'But…' Michaela said, regretting telling him.

'No buts! I'm opening it!'

Mikey Junior rummaged in his pocket, taking out a piece of paper.

'I've got the code for the lock,' Mikey Junior said. 'I memorised it from Solomon's sketchbook and wrote it down.'

He approached the bag, took a deep breath, and began swivelling the dials of the combination lock.

'There!' he said, checking the line up of numbers. 'That should be it!' he said, pulling down the lock.

Michaela was hiding her eyes, not daring to look, unsure whether she wanted the lock to open.

Mikey Junior grinned as the holdall's zip began to move and the bag sat wide open.

'What!' Mikey Junior exclaimed, looking inside and not seeing any money.

Michaela giggled, wiping her runny nose on her sleeve, 'Oops!' she said, more relieved than disappointed.

'Rats! I can't believe it!' Mikey Junior exclaimed, still reeling.

'What is it?' Michaela asked, peering inside, and removing the sunflower halo nestling upon some rocks. They were Todd's rainbow stones, the full set except those from the Blue and Indigo Realms. She held them up to the light, 'no wonder the bag weighed so heavy.'

If she had known the story of how Todd came by the stones, she would have marvelled even more, but they knew nothing about his childhood rainbow adventure.

'Rainbow colours,' Mikey Junior mumbled, thinking more about what to do with the bag.

'So pretty how they sparkle,' Michaela said, not in the least bit disappointed about the money.

'I'd rather have the cash,' Mikey Junior scoffed. 'Pretty stones won't pay for a fancy lawyer.'

'Maybe this will do the trick,' Michaela said, holding up Todd's four-leafed clover paperweight. 'Bring us some good luck. I'm sure we'll think of something,' she said, trying on the sunflower halo.

Her brother snatched it off her head to put on his own. Michaela grabbed it back. 'Suits me better!' she said, sticking out her tongue.

Mikey Junior swiped it again but this time he hurled it like a Frisbee through the air. 'Catch!' he shouted.

Michaela caught it, throwing it back again, her brother catching and returning it. The halo had been back and forth between them a few times, but on the last flight, it dipped, crashing to the ground several feet short of her brother. Mikey Junior picked it up, looking at the battered petals and pressing the sunflowers to reshape them. Suddenly, the halo lit up. Mikey Junior stepped back, dropping it, and squealing as if he had seen a ghost.

'Don't touch it!' he yelled, taking more paces back.

His sister looked confused, 'Don't be sil...' Michaela stopped dead, transfixed by the halo, her mouth wide open.

'Can you see it?' Mikey Junior asked.

Michaela, still stunned and frozen to the spot, took a full minute before she dared to move, trusting enough to take a few steps closer. The halo was on the ground, its largest sunflower staring back at her. Angel Seraphina was smiling.

'What is it?' Michaela asked.

Mikey Junior was still rooted, 'Dunno,' he whispered, 'it's freaking me out!'

Michaela was brave and showed it on the track, overtaking on the inside when others wouldn't dare to see a gap. She took another step forward and reached out to the sunflower's soft petals, so gentle on her skin.

'You're cute!' Michaela whispered, staring into Angel Seraphina's eyes that were like deep pools of sparkling darkness. She picked up the halo and as she touched it, from nowhere, a body appeared to the face: fragile, misty, and otherworldly. Angel Seraphina shimmered above them, a shining beauty, delicate and diaphanous, the sunflower halo glowing above her head.

Mikey Junior had gone for the door, ready to bolt, but Michaela stood still, entranced by the vision before her.

'What happened to you?' Michaela murmured, holding out her hand to the dreamy presence and seeing two shrivelled and drooping wings that looked incapable of flight.

'Stop it!' Mikey Junior snapped, 'it's a frickin freak freaking me out!'

Angel Seraphina reacted, her eyes flickering, but she was still staring.

Mikey Junior opened the stable door, 'let's get the hell outta here!' he said, looking stressed.

'We can't just leave it here! Not with the donkeys!' Michaela said, tugging him back inside to discover that the angel had partially gone. Angel Seraphina's delicate face was still gazing out from the sunflower, but her eyes were dimming until they faded away. Michaela stared at the flower's golden petals and its coffee brown centre, but now there was nothing there. It was just a large sunflower. 'We'll have to hide it,' she said, putting it back into the holdall and covering it with piles of straw.

'What was that?' Mikey Junior exclaimed.

'That, my brother, was a broken Angel!'

Chapter 25

THE POWER
OF TWO

The twins snuck into the farmhouse. It was late, but not so late for anyone to worry. Besides, Todd and Tiggy were hunting for the missing holdall. Nobody suspected that the empty-handed twins knew anything about it, and the children certainly didn't realise that their encounter with Angel Seraphina had endangered them. Todd needed to find it and excused his 'dawn chorus' departure on travelling for 'business', not expecting to be back until the holdall was in his care again. Nobody worked out that the bag was the real reason for Todd's sudden disappearance.

Every morning before school, the twins took their usual walk to the stables, but now, as well as visiting Ned and Nedder Again, they also checked on Todd's holdall and its incredible, secret contents. Michaela referred to it as her 'pet angel'.

'How can it be an angel when it can't even fly?' Mikey Junior asked, still sceptical.

'Well, it certainly isn't human,' Michaela replied, annoyed that she and her twin for once disagreed.

Mikey Junior raised his eyebrows, still doubting her.

'Humans wear knickers! Angels don't!' Michaela said crossly as if it was obvious proof.

'Even if it were true, and a so-called 'pet', you're not taking it for a walk!'

'I might!'

'We'll be bully bait!'

It was exciting and mysterious every time her pet angel's face appeared, but Michaela wished she wasn't broken, and her wings would perk up and fly.

'D'ya think angel power could help us win the UK's?' Michaela asked, smiling as the sunflower's face lit up and Angel Seraphina's face appeared.

'Doubt it! The thing looks weirder than usual today. It looks a bit dead!' Mikey Junior replied, keeping a safe distance.

'Um, maybe she's tired and needs some air.' Angel Seraphina's eyes were fluttering. 'Best let her get some air and sleep!' Michaela said, leaving the holdall unzipped. 'There's always tomorrow.'

The farmhouse had felt flat without Todd around, but with the UK's looming, the focus was intense. After school, Tiggy herded the twins back and forth to the track for extra training and fine-tuning. Robbo was surprisingly winning all the gates; his performance was peaking at the right time, but the twins seemed out of form. It had happened so suddenly: skilful and sharp one week, but without the fast starts and shining moves the next. Tiggy concluded that they were stale and losing their edge, and blamed herself that they may have peaked too soon. Producing champions was such a balancing act between training too much and too little. However, when, later in the week, the school sent them home early feeling unwell, Tiggy called time on their training until they picked up.

It was Sunday leading into a Bank Holiday, and Sapphire had plans with the twins. She arrived at the house full glam, her lips luscious and glossy, strutting in like a supermodel.

'Tell their father to fetch them if you need them at the track. He keeps babbling on about a competition,' she said, trying to push them out of the door. The twins, having rested and feeling brighter, wanted to get back to training.

'We'll be there!' the twins said, giving Tiggy a 'pinky promise'.

Tiggy watched as Sapphire sped away in her shiny sports car, with Bobbi strapped into her baby seat, asleep in the front, and the twins squashed into the back like excess luggage, not wearing their seat belts.

'Where are we going?' Michaela whispered to her brother. 'Bet we're just gonna sit in the car again.'

The glum-faced twins were hoping for the best but expecting the worst. Their mother was only interested in the baby. It was 'Bobbi this' and 'Bobbi that' and 'Hugs (short for Hugh, Bobbi's dad) did this' and 'Hugs did that.' She didn't care about their competition. The twins were a legacy from a past that she wanted to airbrush out of her history.

'Where are we going?' Michaela repeated.

'Bobbi needs you to babysit,' Sapphire said, turning off the engine. She looked in the mirror and smiled, checking her teeth for leaked lipstick.

'Stunner!' she murmured, before letting the twins into the house and taking Bobbi indoors in her portable car seat.

'You know where the nappies are. Bobbi's milk is in the fridge. Warm it as usual,' Sapphire said, picking up two tickets off the kitchen counter and putting them into her expensive-looking handbag. She gave her salon-styled hair a buff up with her brush, popped her designer sunglasses on top of her head and feeling fabulous, went on her way.

'There's Cola and chocolate on the side. Laters!'

Meanwhile, Todd and his campervan were still on a mission against time to find his missing holdall. He'd been on a wild goose chase to the American bases, a player from the London Mets saying he thought he had seen it. However, having drawn a blank, Todd was ready to return to the village and to deal with the consequences. His stomach churned; so much was at stake, he knew that anyone with the holdall could be at risk. Todd drove past the stables without even a glance. He was so tantalisingly close to his bag with the sunflower halo still inside, but at least Ned and Nedder Again hadn't eaten it.

At the track, the Seniors were putting in extra preparation for their UK's a couple of weeks after the Juniors.

'Training when your rivals don't, makes winners. That's why I won. It doesn't happen by chance or magic,' Tiggy called out to the comp squad headed off to the gates. She could hear the surprising but familiar throaty sound of Todd's campervan getting closer. She had missed him, and her heart was racing, expecting him to stop, but he kept on going. Todd passed the track without even glancing, looking as if he had the weight of the world on his shoulders. He knew he should be nourishing the sunflower with The Power of Two; Todd hadn't cared for his Angel in days; she would not survive. He had to find her and find her fast.

However, Todd was not the only one obsessed with his bag. The twins were, too, especially Michaela. They knew they should return it, but Todd hadn't been around.

'I'll give it back 'cos I know you're freaked out by it,' Michaela said, playing 'Peek-a-boo' with Bobbi. The baby was gurgling, raising a clenched hand to touch the soft toy.

'I'm not scared!' Mikey Junior said, trying to act tough.

Michaela giggled, not fooled by her brother. They were twins.

'Yeah, but I'll do it anyway,' she said as they fist bumped.

'D'ya think that thing is one of Todd's dead relatives?' Mikey Junior asked, joining in peek-a-booing Bobbi.

'That 'thing' is my pet angel!' his sister corrected him. 'Maybe, but turned into a kinda broken angel,' Michaela said, giving Bobbi a kiss.

'He'll want it back,' Mikey Junior said, relieved that his sister was chilled about it.

'I'll miss my pet.'

'I'm feeling sick again.'

'Stop worrying!' Michaela said, handing him his Game Boy to take his mind off it. She didn't really believe her brother, although he looked as washed out as the magnolia painted walls.

Back at the stable, Ned and Nedder Again had nosed through the straw and, finding the holdall lying open, sniffed at the sunflower halo. Angel Seraphina's face appeared in the flower's centre. Her smile was weak, and her eyes were dull, closing for a moment and opening wide again, but nobody was there to see apart from the donkeys that, after nosing at the sunflower's petals, decided to give both the bag and the flowers a miss. Angel Seraphina was ailing after several days without the nurture of 'The Power of Two'. She needed Todd, and he needed her, but more crucially, so too, did the twins, except nobody, including Todd, was aware of the jeopardy they faced.

The game consoles gobbled up the time, but midway through the afternoon, Mikey Junior was in a bad way. Michaela, too, was ill. She tried feeding Bobbi her milk but was too queasy to hold the bottle.

'I'm feeling rough...I'm gonna throw up!' Michaela warned. She didn't make it to the toilet in time, and Bobbi, wanting her bottle, started to cry. Within moments, it was pandemonium; Michaela on her knees in a pool of vomit and Mikey Junior slumped on the couch, groaning.

'Ergh, someone help!' Mikey Junior murmured as Michaela crawled over to the telephone. Moments later, he had passed out.

At the track, Tiggy looked at her watch. Her comp squad was there except for the twins. She should have known that their mother taking them in the morning would end in a 'no show' later. Sapphire didn't care. Mikey did, but after his double shift must have overslept and not picked them up. As it happened, this was wrong. Mikey had returned from work, his head barely touching the pillow, before Michaela phoned.

'Micky ...Micky, is that you, sweetheart?' he asked. It was a child's voice, and something wasn't right. 'Micky, Junior, are you there?' but there was no reply. They sounded like they were in trouble.

Mikey grabbed his car keys out of the old ashtray next to the door, racing out of the house in his dressing gown and sped off to his ex's, the home they had shared together until the good times turned rotten.

The house was everything that Sapphire was not: humble, unattractive, and in dire need of a makeover and money spent on it. Sapphire's car wasn't in the driveway, but even metres away, he could hear Bobbi crying. He knocked on all the doors; someone had to be in. Even Sapphire, with her slack parenting, would never leave the baby home alone. Nobody answered, so where were the twins? They should be there. Mikey peered in through the downstairs windows; a bottle of half-empty cola stood on the kitchen worktop, everything looking normal enough, but he could hear Bobbi still crying in another room. The living room curtains were partially drawn but through the gap he could see the baby in her car seat, crying and Michaela slumped in a heap next to her with the phone still in her hand. Mikey would have knocked the door down to get inside, but the spare key was still under the flowerpot by the door where it always used to be.

Chapter 26

HOSPITAL

The old mill's office door was open, and the phone was ringing inside. Tiggy was giving Robbo his racing plate to attach to his bike for the forthcoming UK Championships.

'It's your racing identity. Own it and give it your best!' Tiggy said, still ignoring the phone.

Scotty was hanging around. 'If the twins are still ill or don't show up tomorrow, am I in?' he asked, staring at the racing plate and wishing it were his own. Scotty was an opportunist, something that Tiggy both liked and disliked about him at the same time.

'We'll see,' Tiggy said, heading over to the phone.

It was Mikey. He was gabbling and sounded stressed, his garbled words not making much sense.

'Unconscious?' Tiggy said, having listened for a while.

Mikey had found the twins both slipping in and out of consciousness, unable to communicate, and he had called for an ambulance. The twins were in the hospital, and as he continued speaking, she could hear Bobbi crying in the background.

'Where's Sapphire?' Tiggy asked. Suki and Corey's parents, there to collect them, were hovering; part of the 'sharp-elbowed brigade,' always with a 'can I just' and wanting to 'have a quick word' to benefit their child. Usually, Tiggy didn't mind, it went with the territory, but right now she turned her back, hoping that they would go.

'Home alone?' she questioned. Tiggy frowned. 'I'm coming,' she said, grabbing her keys to lock up for the day.

It was panic stations everywhere: Todd, having unsuccessfully trawled further afield for his holdall, tracking down every player who attended the Open Day, he had returned to the village empty-handed with an air of desperation, hoping that a few days on, somebody would know something to help. He knew it was a long shot, but there was something about Solomon and his otherworldly ways of knowing things that nobody else did that gave Todd hope.

When Tiggy arrived at the hospital, Mikey was pacing with Bobbi asleep in his arms.

'Let me,' Tiggy said, taking the baby from him. 'The twins need you.'

'They're in intensive care,' Mikey said, looking worried and weary, not having slept. 'They've no idea what it is. Damn Sapph!'

'They're in the best place with the best people,' Tiggy said, trying to reassure him as Mikey gnawed every nail on his hands. His leg was jittering up and down; Mikey was a bag of nerves.

'I just want to see them,' he said, walking away to find someone in a uniform to speak to.

The last time that Tiggy had been in this hospital, her father was the patient, rushed in with a head injury that had turned out to be fatal. The moment that Mikey left her, it was like stepping into a time machine and travelling back to that awful 24 hours when her father was fighting for his life. She had always struggled to grasp how someone who was such a force could suddenly fade away and be here one moment and yet, gone the next: That brilliant, mathematical brain and methodical mind, all that knowledge gone in a puff of smoke. It didn't make any more sense or seem any fairer now than it had back then; but that is the point: life is often unfair, people and situations may seem so too, but you should prize each day and make the most of it, whatever that may be. Tiggy looked around her: everything appeared the same as before, the shiny floors, the hustle and bustle in the maze of corridors, the confusing overhead signs, and hidden lifts and stairways. Nothing had changed, and Tiggy reflected on what it all meant; within the hospital's barren walls, lives were born, lost, and sometimes created: the full spectrum of humanity happening right there, under the one roof. The Intensive Care Unit was bringing the memories flooding back of her father's life dangling by a thread until it had not any longer. Bobbi's head was nuzzling against her shoulder as she slept, so contented, so peaceful, and unaware of the tornado of emotions spinning and twisting in Tiggy's head and the big life moments that played out for people in this place every day. Tiggy wandered the corridors to escape the heavy atmosphere in search of a drinks machine or something for a taste of familiarity and home. In that instant, the baby had everything she needed, and as Tiggy felt Bobbi's mouth dribbling, warm, and wet against her shoulder, the miracle of life had never been more acute. She looked at the staff rushing around, members of the public looking purposeful, sometimes sad, worried, or simply bored and killing time whilst they waited. This was it, the circle of life that kept on turning no matter what.

The cafeteria was just like any other work feeding station: lines of utility tables and chairs, and trolleys with trays of dirty plates and dishes. The humdrum of daily routines is so banal, and yet never in sharper focus. On a nearby table, a local newspaper was lying open on a nearly filled-out crossword. Numbers 6 across and 11 down were the blocks to completion. Tiggy hugged her coffee, thumbing through more pages to distract her thoughts from travelling to dark and philosophical places. Bobbi stirred a little and snuggled down again. There wasn't much news and certainly not to set the world alight, but a few pages in, she came to Todd's new baseball club Open Day. As usual, Alicia Gold, the media magnet, had attracted most of the publicity for her disruptive protest on the pitch, but the linked article that followed was alarming; The Local Authority's official notice was there in black and white, confirming the schedule for felling the trees ahead of the proposed developments. The Lightning Tree was on borrowed time. Alicia's stakeout at the tree hadn't lasted long, her followers skipping their turns on the rota with excuses until the idea had dwindled away. Tiggy sipped her coffee, pondering her next move; sometimes life was one big rollercoaster.

Mikey peered through the glass at his children side by side in their beds, separated by vital hospital equipment. Machines lined the walls and IV 'drip' bags hanging from their portable stands, infused the patients via tubes to their wrists, like soldiers standing by for battle. His children looked so small and vulnerable beneath the crisp white sheets, the big space from their feet to the end of the bed underlining it in bold. The recent events had bewildered Mikey, who was completely at a loss as to what had happened. His shifts had robbed him of time with his children, juggling school and the track, and the last occasion they were properly together, the twins had been bursting with energy and bouncing off the walls with excitement for Todd's Open Day, but now this. It was like a nightmare he would eventually wake up from, but knowing that in real time, it was not and he would not. Nurses bustled in and out, checking the monitors, their breathing, and taking their pulse and bloods, and shining lights into their eyes.' It was as if Mikey wasn't there, wasn't important. To the hospital staff, the twins were just two more patients, and yet to Mikey, they were his world. They were just busy being busy, but Mikey felt overwhelmed by this waiting game to find out more. There were so many questions needing answers, and from Sapphire, who had just arrived.

'What's going on?' she asked, raising her sunglasses and perching them on the top of her glossy hair. She looked through the glass at the twins, their eyes closed, motionless in their beds, and attached to so many tubes that her mischievous children looked more like a scientific experiment.

'I could ask you the same,' Mikey replied, shocked by the front of this woman that, for the first time, he now genuinely felt happy to be his ex. Sapphire had always been a bad apple, except he just hadn't known it. Mikey was reeling. He had been many things in his past, but he was a good, solid, and loving dad to his twins.

'It is what it is and what's done is done,' she said unapologetically. 'They just need to get better.' Sapphire was only worried about covering for herself. 'None of this is my fault. You do know that?' she said, staring at Mikey with steely eyes hoping he would engage. He looked away, shaking his head in disgust at her detachment from the part she had played. 'Who's got Bobbi?' she asked, 'Where is she?'

'She's fine!' said Tiggy, walking up to them with Bobbi cradled in her arms. 'Is there any news?'

Tiggy looked at Mikey's beaten face, the worry and sadness of his 'dadness' written in every line and expression as Sapphire stood wrong and strong.

Mikey shook his head. 'It has to be something they've drunk or eaten; it's both of them.' He looked at Sapphire, wanting answers, 'Have you been using again? I thought you were clean?'

'I am clean. You know I am,' Sapphire replied dismissively. 'It looks like they're sleeping it off.'

She pressed her nose to the glass and sighed at the motionless figures beneath the bed covers.

'They're not sleeping it off,' Mikey barked. 'They're in a coma. This is on you!'

✹✹✹✹✹✹✹✹✹✹✹✹

The following day's weather was 'decentish,' with the emphasis on the '-ish' due to the threat of some storms later, all the standard Bank Holiday jeopardy for outdoor plans. First thing, the sky was OK, cloudy with nothing too menacing amongst the cloud formations, and so the annual Bank Holiday ECM picnic was going ahead on the surrounding meadows: tartan blankets, cool bags, lunch boxes, and hampers marked each family's territory amongst the buttercups and daisies for the fresh air family feast. Nathan had lined up his dinosaurs with great precision around the edge of his family's picnic blanket, securing their space before Nathan would agree to eat. However, with his collection, including Stegosaurus, standing neatly in alphabetical order, Nathan was enjoying a cheese and strictly smooth pickle sandwich when Nureyev swung by. The greyhound had picked his spot, flopping down onto the rug, and knocking over several of the plastic figures. Nathan growled and shouted, scrapping up to reposition his dinosaurs to regain his sense of order, but in his panic to put things right, some of his dinosaurs wouldn't stand up and toppled over again. Nathan was angry. His family had seen it all before and rallied to help, but when his Diplodocus was missing, Nathan kicked over the cool box in frustration and burst into tears. His mother held him tight, hoping to calm him and to find the Diplodocus quickly. Nathan's little sister with her head down, looking glum, stepped a few paces away from this familiar scene. Fortunately, the crisis was soon over when Nureyev moved off the rug, revealing the missing dinosaur.

If only they could find the lost holdall as easily. When Todd arrived, a game of Hide and Seek was about to start. It was 'Daisy's game' with her choosing herself to be the first to hide. Solomon was sitting cross-legged beside his mother, drawing in his sketchpad not wanting to join in. He had sketched two pictures: the picnic, and another of the donkeys in their stables. It didn't take long for the seekers to find Daisy buried beneath a pile of waterproofs, having left her feet sticking out. Now that Todd was there, Solomon had changed his mind about playing and wanting to hide, he joined his thumbs and index fingers to make his customary parting 'love heart' for his mother.

'I love you too!' Tanisha responded smiling at her son as Todd scanned the bags on the picnic blankets for his holdall. He wasn't really in the mood for games; nobody had seen his bag, and it had been a week since the Open Day. However, if anyone could lead him to his holdall, it would be Solomon. He had extraordinary powers, like a third eye that could see every secret, including thoughts. There was something remarkable about him, and as the ECM seekers counted aloud to a hundred, Todd and Solomon headed off to hide. It was around this time that Tiggy contacted Penelope with the worrying news about the twins. Theo heard it all. He loved anything medical and the more scientific, the better.

Solomon thrust his drawing of the stables at Todd, not hesitating or deviating from his chosen hiding place for even a second. He led Todd straight to the stables and pointed inside.

'You want to hide?' Todd whispered.

Solomon shook his head. He had no intention of hiding. He knew why Todd was there and how much the holdall mattered.

'Coming, ready or not!' the ECM seekers called out, their voices muffled, some distance away.

Todd closed the stable door, waking up Ned and Nedder Again, who were dozing on their feet, but seeing that they had company, the donkeys nudged up to them for attention. However, Solomon hadn't taken Todd there either to hide or for the donkeys. He walked around the stable and then began to burrow into the piles of straw.

✳ ✳ ✳ ✳ ✳ ✳ ✳ ✳ ✳ ✳ ✳ ✳

Overnight at the hospital things had taken a turn for the worse. The patients were wearing oxygen masks, and the word coma was on everyone's lips, including their consultant. The twins were not responding to voices, bright lights, or pain, but the tests were inconclusive as to the cause or the extent of any damage. Toxic substances were not the cause whether drugs, high street medications, or alcohol. The consultant assessed their condition as critical, and whilst both children were in the danger zone, Michaela was causing the most concern. Her breathing was irregular even with the oxygen mask. The consultant scratched her head, studying the monitors, and leaning over the patients, she shone a bright light into their eyes, taking a closer look. She had never had a case like this before. She needed answers and fast as the children's conditions were deteriorating by the hour.

Mikey paced up and down, having drunk tea and coffee on tap. He hugged his cup for comfort, but there was none. In the evening, Sapphire had taken Bobbi home, but Tiggy had stayed at Mikey's side all night. The boy who had once bullied Alex had matured and mended his ways; he had proved his worth and become a good friend. He didn't deserve what was happening here, and neither did his twins. For now, Tiggy wouldn't be going anywhere. She had grown close to the twins and loved them despite their challenging and sometimes misguided behaviour, and it cut her deeply that Mikey's usually boisterous children looked so fragile through the glass.

'May I see them?' Mikey asked a nurse breezing past them on her way into the room.

'Maybe later,' the nurse replied, barely giving him a glance. She didn't mean it. He would be in their way.

All through the night, Mikey watched the monitor from the window, tracking the coloured squiggles across the screen and predicting the next spike. He would have breathed for them if he could. Never had he felt so helpless, but there was a weird kind of comfort in watching the lines, giving himself a purpose in the battle against time. Mikey's charged emotions had drained him and shattered from lack of sleep, only the adrenaline rush kept him awake as he urged the monitors to stay within their safe zones. The minutes rolled into hours, but as the new day dawned, there was no improvement in their condition.

'What if they never come out of this coma?' Mikey asked.

Tiggy shrugged, struggling to find the right thing to say, 'Just keep on believing. Those kids are tough, the toughest I know,' she said, patting his knee.

Mikey nodded, but he was fighting back the tears.

'It's OK not to be OK. Let them fall!' she whispered, giving his hand a squeeze. Mikey sobbed. The twins had taken him to a place and stirred up emotions unlike any he had ever had before and as he paced up and down the corridor, he started to pray despite not having been in a church since his primary school nativity when he was a shepherd with a tea towel on his head, in a makeshift stable.

❁ ❁ ❁ ❁ ❁ ❁ ❁ ❁ ❁ ❁ ❁

However, right now in a stable in Great Snubington, another story was unfolding; when a crisis strikes, turning your world upside down or smashing it to smithereens, somewhere, somebody else will be having a shining moment: that someone was Solomon. While the twins were fighting for their lives, he was triumphantly throwing straw into the air, having glimpsed something red. It was Todd's missing holdall.

'Jeez! You knew it was here. Dude, you have a superpower!' Todd said, shaking Solomon's hand and pulling the bag clear of the straw.

Solomon's top lip crinkled, turning up at its corners; he loved impressing Todd. However, Todd's euphoria had already evaporated: the bag was open and not as he had left it. Somebody had tampered with the holdall and hidden it in the stable. A tornado whirled in Todd's head, his mind in turmoil: how was Angel Seraphina without The Power of Two? Who had taken the bag and put themselves at risk? Was it time he returned to the rainbow to face the Wobniar and for Solomon to pitch for that life-saving home run? Was he about to leave Tiggy again after searching for her for so long? Todd looked into the bag, fearful of what he would see: his rainbow crystals were there, and the sunflower halo, but the petals were dull and crispy, the heads drooping as at the end of the flowering season. Todd knew that whilst he felt fine, Angel Seraphina clearly was not. Holding the sunflower halo in his hands, he tenderly stroked the petals for what seemed like an eternity, waiting for her to appear. This time it was different. Seraphina was struggling to break through: her eyes were dim and barely open, her wan smile fading away; she was hanging on by a thread. There could be no more time to waste. This was it, the end game; Todd tucked the crystals inside his pockets and ran out into the sunlight to set in motion The Power of Two, but Seraphina was so weak that she seemed beyond its nurture.

'Whoever took the holdall will also be in danger,' Todd mumbled. Solomon sat down and started to draw.

✿✿✿✿✿✿✿✿✿✿✿✿

Just before midday, Sapphire returned to the hospital and sat with Mikey outside the twins' room. He looked at her immaculately made-up face, false lashes, and perfectly straightened hair, knowing that looking good had won over having precious time with her children. Nevertheless, they papered over the cavernous cracks in their relationship, knowing they would be lucky if there was a custody battle still left to fight. Tiggy, sensing the awkwardness, escaped to the cafeteria for another round of tea drinking therapy.

The twins were under close surveillance, but suddenly Michaela's apparatus had started to beep, and three more nurses entered the room. They crowded the monitors, and speaking in coded instructions, they sprang into action like well-oiled machinery, each with a different task. The word had spread, more staff rushing into the room, as the waves on Michaela's monitor were erratic. Her bed was their focus, but with the twins' symptoms so far mirroring each other's, it seemed likely that Mikey Junior's condition would shadow his sister's, and two more nurses were on standby. Mikey's eyes, charged with fear, flashed at Sapphire.

'I must see them. I must be there,' he roared, barging into the room. 'I'm their father. They need me!' Mikey was physically tired and emotionally exhausted.

A nurse firmly gripped his arm, trying to calm him. 'Please! Let us do our best to help your children.'

In the cafe, it was quiet, and the newspaper was still on the same table open on the crossword page and remained incomplete, although somebody had solved the clue to '11 down.' Tiggy looked at the clue for '6 across' and its completed letters: 'Type of angel,' she murmured, 'Seraphina, you l'il beauty!' and scribbling 'Seraph' into the blank boxes, the puzzle was done. She wished they could solve the twins' puzzling diagnosis as easily. She thought about the twins and their feuding parents, her mind briefly drifting back to Todd, who had driven past her yesterday without stopping by to chat. He had been gone for a week, and she hadn't heard from him since; time would tell if he had changed his mind, but all that really mattered was that the twins got better. They just had to for anything to seem worthwhile.

However, as Tiggy took her time, calmly sipping her tea, in contrast, upstairs in ICU there was a controlled but frantic urgency: Mikey Junior's condition had mimicked Michaela's, and as the monitors beeped and the lights on the screen flashed, everyone was on high alert and on task.

Mikey having fought to stay in the room had at least briefly held their hands. So much was playing out in his head: happy stories from their past, making promises and plans, and declaring his love for the twins in the present. Nothing focuses the mind and crystallises thoughts and feelings more than when life is teetering on the brink.

'Hang in there, kids! Please stay!' Mikey pleaded, looking desperate and partway broken, rooting for his children.

THE HOME RUN

Any day on this fair island is not truly bank holiday worthy without at least a smidgen of rain, and by late afternoon, spits and spots had started to fall, but with rain ponchos on standby it wasn't going to dampen the picnickers' spirits.

'Are you sure about this?' Todd asked, staring at Solomon's drawings. 'The twins hid my bag?'

Solomon nodded. A chill slithered down Todd's spine; apart from the track, the donkey stable was one of the twins' favourite places. Solomon was never wrong; his sixth sense always served him well. Todd looked at Angel Seraphina's sickly face, her drooping petals, and fading eyes, giving up the fight. Soon they would close forever, and in that heart-sinking moment, he knew that the twins' lives must also be in danger. It was time. He zipped up the holdall, looking up at the sky, and headed to the baseball field with Solomon in pursuit.

'Gotcha!' shouted an excited Daisy, spinning around and trying to handstand to celebrate finding them. Her friends, not far behind, joined in; Leeroy punched the air, Harry and Sophie high-fived Daisy, unaware that she hadn't really found Todd and Solomon at all.

'Adam says the twins are in hospital,' Theo announced, throwing a ball up into the air to catch.

'He told you that?' Todd questioned picking up a baseball bat and swishing it through the grass.

Theo nodded, 'Yep! They're both in intensive care.'

'Are they going to die?' asked Daisy.

'Probably,' Theo said, not looking as upset as he should be. 'The ICU stats for fatalities are pretty high. Everyone knows that.'

Daisy whimpered and looked scared.

'They're in good hands,' Todd reassured her.

'How do you know if hands are good or bad?' Daisy asked, staring at her own.

'What I meant was that I'm sure the twins will be OK, Daisy,' Todd explained, but a million thoughts were bombing around in his head to the contrary.

He looked long and hard at Solomon, who stared back as if they were transmitting thoughts to each other with a silent understanding, 'Remember what I've taught you,' he said, handing Solomon a ball, ' pitch long, and high enough for me to hit it. I need to score a home run.'

Solomon's face was expressionless, but there was plenty going on in his head.

'You can do this, Dude!' Todd said with a fist bump as he firmly placed the sunflower halo onto his own head. He hesitated and then, before walking away to the home plate, he whispered into Solomon's ear, 'Tell Tiggy I love her.'

This was the moment of reckoning. Everything was set; Todd poised himself in the batter's box, ready to strike. Daisy's group stood at the bases waiting to field the ball, clapping, gradually faster and louder as Solomon prepared to pitch.

In the hospital, the outlook was bleak. Although nobody knew it, the twins were counting on Todd, and Todd was counting on Solomon and his friends.

Solomon stared down the home plate at Todd, his target, taking aim whilst Todd planted his stance, poised to receive.

'Down, back, around, and up through and release,' Todd called out, but after several failed attempts, Solomon's arm was getting tired. The time was approaching half past four in the afternoon, the rain had turned into a heavy shower, and although everyone was getting wet, it didn't dampen the enthusiasm.

'Sol-o-mon! Sol-o-mon! Sol-o-mon!' Daisy chanted, with everyone else then joining in. A special energy was in the air, the energy of a shared mission amongst friends.

'Again!' Todd called out. 'This time's the one!'

Solomon didn't react, but for the first time he felt that he belonged, the support boosting him with a sudden injection of vim and vigour, his arm like a propeller, swinging around and around before launching the ball...this time, it was on a good trajectory for Todd to strike. The connection between the bat and ball was perfect.

'Take me with you!' an unknown voice called out. The voice belonged to Solomon who had spoken for the first time, but the ball had already orbited the air and into the brilliant sunshine that had burst through following the rain.

'Look at the rainbow!' Daisy shouted. It was dazzlingly blinding, unlike any rainbow they had ever seen before, and whilst everyone squinted, shading their eyes in wonder, Todd disappeared as if he had only ever been a figment of their imagination.

✱ ✱ ✱ ✱ ✱ ✱ ✱ ✱ ✱ ✱ ✱ ✱

At the hospital, Mikey had been praying for a miracle. The consultant's grim assessment had left Mikey hoping for the best but expecting the worst. If the twins' inexplicable deterioration continued at the same rate, they were unlikely to make it through another night. However, against the odds, and after several successful emergency interventions over the next few hours, the pandemonium around the beeping and flashing screens calmed. That afternoon, Penelope had left the picnic early and bustled into the hospital, putting her umbrella down. For a while, the rain was torrential, a localised cloudburst by all accounts.

'I came straight away when you weren't at home. I thought you'd be here,' Penelope said, trying to get a read on the situation.

'What's the news on the twins?' she asked.

'Mikey found them yesterday, collapsed and unconscious, home alone with the baby. They're in a coma and it's not looking good.'

Penelope shook her head, 'How awful! Poor Mikey!'

The corridor leading to the twins' room had a heavy, sombre atmosphere, and every passing face matched the mood. Tiggy strolled over to a nearby window for a glimpse of daylight and a ray of hope after so long cooped up within the bland, beige warren that did nothing to lift the spirits. She watched as people moved around the car park, taking great care to step over and walk around the huge puddles. In that moment, the puddles seemed to be all that mattered to them. Hospitals are such a prime location for highlighting perspective. A little girl splashed her way through a big puddle, much to her mother's annoyance, treating it like a major disaster. Tiggy smiled, knowing that the wet feet would dry. There are big dramas and little dramas, but so often, we confuse the two. The rain, at least, had now completely stopped, and the sun was breaking through again.

Suddenly, Mikey appeared from the door several yards up the corridor. He looked excited, his tired, dull eyes shining with a brightness not seen since he had been there. It was the brightness of hope. The twins' eyes had flickered, and they were stirring in their beds: they were both coming out of their coma, and remarkably at the same time. Nurses and consultants stared at the patients, amazed by what was happening, and as the news spread through the corridors, more staff gathered, curious to see the rapid change in the twins who were now sitting up in bed, wondering what all the fuss was about and what they were doing there. Tiggy looked at the clock on the wall. It was 4.30 p.m., and although she was unaware, it was the same time as Todd had struck the ball for the home run.

Chapter 28

THE UK CHAMPIONSHIPS

Tiggy and Penelope left the hospital with their hearts lifted and bursting with good feelings. They, too, gingerly dodged the puddles in the car park but missed seeing the beautiful rainbow that had dazzled Great Snubington several minutes earlier. The twins were an unsolved mystery, and nobody, including the medical staff, understood why the twins were critically ill, fighting to survive one moment and fighting fit the next. None of it made sense. How could anyone possibly have known the key part the theft of an ordinary-looking holdall had played in putting the twins in their hospital beds?

'I guess you know that Todd's back?' Penelope queried.

Tiggy nodded. 'He drove straight past me at the track as if I didn't exist.'

'Don't take it personally. It'll be that missing bag of his. He was still looking for it at the picnic.'

'Kinda weird don't you think? Who gets that worked up about losing an old bag?' Tiggy responded

Penelope shrugged, 'Depends what's inside it. Whatever it is, he looked worried. Todd's nuts about you, though.'

Tiggy wasn't convinced and despite the excellent news about the twins, she was giving miserable in her face, demeanour, and flat voice. Her last meal was two days ago, but she had no appetite and nothing much to say. Penelope hoped she was right about Todd and that he wasn't just another Gav who talked a good story but was all fiction. However, as they approached the house, the mood in the car lifted, discovering Todd's campervan already there.

'See! He's home! You've been worrying for nothing,' Penelope said as she dropped her sister outside her door.

Tiggy was bursting to see Todd: she had so much news to share. It had been quite a week. However, the moment the key turned in the door and opened to stony silence, Tiggy knew that Todd wasn't there. All she could do was wait for him and hope. Buddy nuzzled up to her, sensitive to her mood, knowing that Tiggy needed him.

'You're my Number 1, Buddy. You've never let me down,' she said, stroking his velvety ears and giving him a hug. The Labrador was Tiggy's constant, the one thing that she could count on. He was always pleased to see her and, holding onto him, melting into his soft fur, she instantly felt a bit better.

Todd, Mikey and the twins had certainly brought a new energy to the farmhouse, albeit noisy and chaotic, but now with just Buddy at her side again, the place didn't feel right, as if something was missing, like a living room without a sofa and the things that made a place a home. Todd, Mikey, and the twins were now on that list, and she wanted them back.

Tiggy looked out of the window and reflected on recent events. Thankfully, the twins had recovered and if all remained well could be home in less than 48 hours. The last she had heard they were playing 'eye spy' and asking for their Game Boys. Todd's campervan was still outside, and yet he would normally have left for work by now. Something didn't feel right, and peering around Todd's bedroom door, his suit was there on the hanging rail and his work shoes by his bed. He said he was going on a business course, but now it seemed shady. She had thought that she could trust him, but her mind was in overdrive, fabricating a double life for Todd. She knew the chilled, baseball Todd that bombed around 'Snubs' in his campervan, but could he, somewhere else, be a different Todd with another circle of people? His past, shrouded in mystery, had many blank pages that might explain it. Tiggy had gone into the bank holiday weekend with clarity for the UK Championships and life afterwards with Todd, but had come out of it with everything blurred. It is that well-trodden path and expression that life is what happens to you when you are busy making plans.

The following day Todd had still not turned up or been back to his campervan. He'd left it unlocked: an open can of Irn-Bru was on the dashboard and the radio playing on low volume. It seemed to confirm that something must have happened suddenly, and then Penelope called her with news.

Her sister sounded serious. 'The kids are saying some crazy stuff. They reckon Todd just vanished, playing baseball with them one second and gone the next.'

'How d'ya mean 'vanished?''

'Daisy didn't seem to know. She just kept going on about seeing a rainbow and Todd disappearing. Don't laugh! She reckons the rainbow swallowed him up!'

Tiggy was certainly not laughing, 'Go on...,' she said, wanting to hear more.

'Theo has completely clammed up. He says, and I quote, 'something unexpected and improbable happened, but I do not understand the science,' unquote.'

Tiggy's eyes narrowed, mulling things over in her head, 'Really?'

'That's honestly what they said, but you know what Daisy's like ...she makes stuff up all the time, whilst Theo's the opposite: he won't say anything about anything that he can't explain with science and facts.'

There was a lot to unpack, giving Tiggy lots to think about, including the final two training sessions prior to the UK championships. Scotty was first reserve, desperate to be part of the action, and had kept hanging around, eager to have his place confirmed. However, when Tiggy got to the track, not only was Scotty there early, but Mikey and the twins were there, too, beaming from ear to ear.

'Surprise, surprise!' they chorused. 'We're back!'

'The hospital has discharged them with a clean bill of health. The consultant said they're fine to compete,' Mikey said, looking years younger than the last time she had seen him. 'She's calling them, 'The Miracle'.'

Scotty looked gutted, but trying not to show it, slinked away to be on his own.

Tiggy grinned, 'We'd best get to work then! Starting gates, you lot!'

Tiggy and Mikey's eyes said it all. They had forged a strong bond over the twins and would now always be there for each other.

Later that day, Tiggy checked on Todd's campervan to see if he'd been back to it whilst she'd been away. He hadn't, and there was no sign of him but the twins' excitement about being home and the UK's at the weekend deflected from her disappointment.

'Where's Todd?' they asked, looking in his bedroom. 'I bet he's with Solomon.'

'I wish he was with Solomon,' Tiggy replied, 'He's had to go away for a bit.'

'Awh!' Mikey Junior said, settling down to play on his Game Boy. They would soon stop missing Todd; life moved on quickly in their world.

✺ ✺ ✺ ✺ ✺ ✺ ✺ ✺ ✺ ✺ ✺ ✺

The following day was 'chippy tea Friday'. Finally, with the arduous work done preparing her budding BMX champions, Tiggy headed to the fish and chip shop. Solomon was hanging around at the baseball park looking sad and at a loose end. She knew that he was hoping to see Todd.

'I'm missing Todd, too. Do you know where he is? Tiggy asked, her eyes probing, hoping that Solomon would give something away with his face. For once, he stared straight back, looking into her eyes. Solomon knew something. He dropped his head and walked away clutching a baseball that Todd had given him. Maybe in time he would find a way to tell.

Tiggy rose early the next morning. It was time to shine for her UK competition squad. After recent events, it was a bonus for the twins even being at the championships, but with such fine margins between the best, it would not be surprising if their good fortune had run out. Scotty, who had gone to watch as first reserve, wasn't happy.

'I should be out there. The twins'll never come back from death's door to win, and Robbo shouldn't be there over me anyway. I could beat the lot of them!' he grumbled loud enough for Tiggy to hear.

MJ and Robbo were determined to prove him wrong. Sharp reflexes, power, and nerve had advanced them through their heats and semi-finals. Robbo was on fire, winning every gate and had aced his semi-final, but he hadn't raced against MJ yet, who had placed second in his. Nevertheless, Robbo was looking a bit of a dark horse and a real contender for the title.

'Come on boys!' Tiggy shouted, hardly bearing to watch.

The finalists were ready: backs set up straight, wrists high, stance alert with their front wheel pressed against the starting gates, primed for them to drop. The wait was tense, the atmosphere electric. This was it, a single race to crown the champion, hundreds of hours of hard work and sacrifice, boiling down to their outcome within the next few seconds. Everyone was willing an explosive start, but only one rider from the eight would win the gate and pole position, gaining the clearest, unhindered view of the obstacles ahead.

The gate dropped, and true to form, Robbo won the starting gate and was out in front, his legs pumping, the bike eating up the course. Taking the bends and mastering the jumps with MJ spearheading the pack, chasing Robbo down. The title was there for the taking, Robbo looking imperious within touching distance of victory, but with only a couple more obstacles to go, Tiggy let out an agonising yell from the stand, knowing that it was all about to go horribly wrong. She spotted the fault, in motion, before the consequence played out: taking the penultimate jump, Robbo landed nose first, flipping him over the handlebars, and taking MJ clean out a mere split second later. Both boys and two more of the front-runners were down and out in the biggest pile-up of the event, with the leading back runner crossing the line to steal the victory and glory. Tiggy's eyes were on her boys until they were back on their feet and walking away, hopefully without more than a few bruises between them. Scotty wiped away a little grin with his hand, relieved not to be feeling jealous after all.

'Always next year,' Tiggy said loud enough for Suki to hear. Suki's dismal performance in her heats was lacklustre: left at the gate and trailing at the back, she had finished last in the qualifying rounds. Nevertheless, Micky had made it through to the final and was still flying the flag for BMX Mania. She had watched the carnage on the track and the disappointing ending for the boys, but she and MJ had come through worse, much worse. Crashed bikes and debris cleared away, the Junior Girls' final loomed. Micky prepared, getting into the zone; this was her time. The adrenaline was pumping through her veins, her body on fire, as the butterflies built. It was pressure, but after her recent hospital saga, she gladly received the uncomfortable feeling as a privilege. She focussed on the track, shutting out the noise to let her mind do the rest.

Micky had lost out at the gate in her semi-final and had trailed by too far to overtake, but she relished being the underdog at the starting gates. Contests like this are so often won or lost in the mind. Just days before, she had been in a coma and an underdog to survive, so having battled out of it, her body and mind had to be strong, proving that underdogs could win.

Nervous energy fed her primed body and as the gates dropped, Tiggy clenched her fists, holding her breath.

MJ and Robbie, dusted down and nursing a few bruises, snuck in beside her just in time to watch the final, willing their team-mate on.

Micky exploded into action out of the gate, vying for the lead with the race favourite in the next lane. Both girls were out in front by a clear margin giving it everything. They were the race masters, their superior skills, power, and sharp reactions coming to the fore and leaving the field behind. Whether a banked corner, jump or roller, they matched each other with their smooth landings, fast lines, and ferocious speed on the straights; it was either girl's race, and the noisy crowd were on their feet as the race leaders were neck and neck coming into the last section. One split-second decision going into the last corner, Micky took the tightest entry line, braking late to come out ahead. In the blink of an eye, Micky sprinted over the line to win.

Two days later, there was more good news when an official-looking letter arrived for Mikey.

'Sapph has called off the dogs and dropped the custody battle for the twins,' Mikey grinned, showing Tiggy the letter.

'She knew she'd never win,' said Tiggy, 'leaving young children home alone with a baby; she's lucky you haven't got the police involved.'

'I can't wait to tell them. What a difference a week makes!'

'Yeah, you're right!' Tiggy agreed, feeling happy for Mikey but not for herself. It was a week since Todd had disappeared and there was still no sign of him. So much had happened: the twin's mystery illness and miraculous recovery, Mikey winning his custody battle and Michaela becoming UK Champion. How she wished she had Todd there to share it with, but the clock keeps ticking and life goes on.

Chapter 29

SAVING THE LIGHTNING TREE

The development plans to change their sleepy village were ironically causing sleepless nights for some of the Great Snubington residents.

The revered Lightning Tree would soon be for the chop. Tiggy had heard rumblings in the village that the plans to save it had failed, but Alicia was adamant there would be no surrendering to the chainsaw and diggers, and an appeal was in progress. It was such a mighty tree and landmark, steeped in the village's history, that it deserved an official preservation order. Arthur Ramsbottom had hoped his memorial to the curse victims would secure its protection, but as far as the council were concerned, it was 'unofficial' and did not count. They were the rule and decision makers that everyone else had to stick to, and their job was to ensure that they did.

'Please don't let anything happen to it without me being there,' Arthur kept saying.

Tiggy had promised. The tree was everything to Arthur. It was sacred and should be untouchable.

Alicia and a few of her followers were already there and Timothy Grimshaw was about to join them, pushing his wife in her wheelchair over the uneven ground.

'For heaven's sake, Timothy, you'll make me bring up my breakfast! You know how scrambled eggs and kippers repeat on me!' Gertie moaned as the wheelchair bumped over a series of mounds.

'Park her right beneath the tree!' instructed Alicia. 'If a disabled, grumpy, ratbag old woman doesn't stop them cutting it down, nothing will.'

Gertie looked daggers but didn't say a word.

'And they'll have me to contend with!' Alicia said unfolding a camping chair and planting herself on it as if she intended to take root there.

'Chain me to the tree!' she ordered Timothy, handing him a padlock and chain. 'I can't believe they haven't accepted my little financial incentive,' she said, shaking her head, 'it usually works!'

Gertie Grimshaw, on a personal mission to make jumpers for her gnomes, took out her knitting and prepared for a long vigil. She could be tough as old boots when needed. The word was that the tree surgeon and council bods would turn up 'out of hours' to catch out the protesters. They weren't due for two days, but Alicia wasn't taking any chances.

'It's a setup. They'll come earlier than the date they've said, and once the tree is down, there's nothing anyone can do about it.' Alicia announced, confident she was right. 'They think they're so clever; I'd say sly, and arrogant. They're the ones who need cutting down to size.'

For once, Tiggy and Arthur agreed with Alicia, staying within earshot whilst keeping their distance.

'Feisty!' Arthur commented, happy that the village's usual thorn in the side was doing something useful.

'I've organised a rota with round-the-clock surveillance. They won't catch us napping!' Alicia bleated.

'I didn't think I'd ever see the day I'd be rooting for Alicia to pull off one of her media stunts. The papers are going to love this!' Arthur chuckled.

Tiggy nodded, 'As long as your tree survives, she can be as mad as she likes!'

Later that same day, Tiggy was at the track throwing a celebration party for their new UK champion.

She was so proud of her little track star, 'Miracle Micky'.

'It was a cinch thanks to you, Miss,' Michaela said, smiling at her coach. 'After all that hospital stuff, I knew I could beat anything or anyone.'

Rach and Beryl on the late shift at the tree were throwing their own party, blasting out the Take That numbers so loudly that they could hear them at the track. Bo squirmed at her mother's antics.

'My Mum kills me!' she said, blushing. 'She's so embarrassing!'

Nobody cared. Everyone was there to party, although not necessarily to celebrate Micky's success. 'The Girls' were jealous and determined to steal any male attention and dull her limelight; they were hanging out with 'The Lads.' The Swiss, as usual, were the go-betweens for the cliques, never taking sides, but stirring up trouble between them, whilst Scotty and Suki consoled each other, putting a plaster on their championships' wound. The party was in full swing, and Tiggy was setting off party poppers when Penelope and Nureyev arrived. They had Solomon with them.

'Just came to congratulate the new UK champion,' she said. The Macarena was playing, and everyone except Mikey Junior was joining in with the dance. He was curious and nosy, wanting to be first to find out stuff and he was hoping to hear some news about Todd.

'Solomon was at the ballpark, presumably waiting for Todd,' Penelope said, feeling sorry for Solomon, who looked so sad. Mikey Junior started sulking; it was always 'Solomon this and Solomon that'. They spoke of him as if he was a saint. Mikey Junior didn't know the crucial part Solomon had played in their cure. It was because of him that they were now 'The Miracle'.

'My hunch is he'll be waiting a long time!' whispered Tiggy behind her hand, blocking her mouth.

In fact, Solomon had visited the baseball field every day, hoping to find Todd.

'I can't believe he's just vanished,' Penelope said. 'People and things don't usually just disappear without a logical explanation.'

'His bag did!' Tiggy contradicted.

'It didn't,' Penelope responded, 'Solomon found it, didn't you, Solomon?'

Solomon nodded. Tiggy willed him to speak, but he hadn't spoken since Todd hit the home run.

Mikey Junior couldn't bear it any longer. 'I found it first!' he butted in wanting the glory, miffed about 'Saint Solomon'.

Solomon didn't react but instead fumbled in his pocket, producing Todd's four-leafed clover paperweight, holding it out for Tiggy.

Tiggy stared, cupping it in her hands like a most precious gift.

'That was all that was in the bag,' Penelope said.

Solomon nodded again, but Mikey Junior was irritated, 'Nah, you're wrong! There were coloured stones and a weird sunflower thing. Micky and I played Frisbee with it.'

Tiggy froze. She stared at the paperweight, so many memories flashing through her head: she was that Rainbow Child once more. It was such a long time ago, but the feelings were still as powerful now as they were back then; in The Realms again, remembering the Stig Man's big, bolted smile when she gave him the four-leaf clover.

'Surely not!' she mumbled under her breath.

❋ ❋ ❋ ❋ ❋ ❋ ❋ ❋ ❋ ❋ ❋ ❋

The next morning, the vigil at the tree continued. Tiggy and Arthur, with Buddy off lead, arrived to find one unholy mess the night crew had left behind, and that Alicia was back on shift.

'Dear oh dear,' said Arthur poking his walking stick at some empty cans and manoeuvring it to scoop up a discarded crisp packet.

Tiggy had picked up most of the rubbish when she suddenly became aware that Alicia, her family's old enemy, was smiling at her.

'This must be awful for you,' Alicia said, looking concerned at Arthur. It seemed sincere.

Arthur nodded. 'This tree feels a part of me,' he agreed. 'Thanks for trying so hard to save it.'

'And we will. Hugo Uppingham is representing us at the appeal. The man has worked his socks off to find loopholes and build a defence. He's clever and he's confident.'

'Do you really think there's a chance?' Tiggy asked amazed to be having an actual civil conversation with Alicia Gold, but she was.

'We'll win! We 'Snubers' are made of the right stuff!' Alicia said, holding out an olive branch to Tiggy and calling a truce on their years of hostility and animosity. The two women shook hands, drawing an invisible line in the sand.

By late afternoon, there was still no sign of the feared diggers and men with chainsaws. Tiggy wanted answers to the questions she had about Todd, and so, on her way to the track, she called in at Every Child Matters to speak to Daisy. She was one of the very last people to have seen him.

Daisy was in the Lego Room building a stable for Sky Skimmer, her newest 'My Little Pony.'

'Solomon threw the ball, and Todd whacked it so hard into the sky the ball got lost in a big bright rainbow,' Daisy said, continuing to build with the blocks.

'Go on...' Tiggy said, encouraging her and passing her some more bricks.

'It was so bright I thought I'd gone blind,' Daisy said, placing her pony inside her unfinished stable.' She had no idea of the enormity of what she was saying.

'And...?' Tiggy prompted.

'And then Todd had gone. The rainbow swallowed him up,' Daisy said as if it was nothing, more interested in her pony's new home.

Tiggy could feel the four-leafed clover paperweight in her pocket, her thoughts drifting back to her rainbow adventures with the Stig Man, the trapped Rainbow Child. He had a mass of tangled dreadlocks, Todd had a shaved scalp, but they were both American baseball nuts...

❉ ❉ ❉ ❉ ❉ ❉ ❉ ❉ ❉ ❉ ❉ ❉

The following day was the designated date for the felling of the Lightning Tree. Arthur had dreaded this day for a long time, and the night before hadn't slept a wink; the terrible storm seventy years earlier, when he had lost his twin Arnold, was playing on a loop in his head. However, coincidentally, the village had had thunder and heavy rain overnight that had kept many of the villagers awake. The long, lush grass was soaking wet, and the ground was muddy with lots of puddles, but the villagers were undeterred, arriving in large numbers determined to sabotage any attempts to sever the mighty oak. Arthur and Tiggy arrived arm in arm, with Buddy doing his own thing on his familiar home turf.

'How could they even think about cutting you down?' Arthur wailed to the tree. 'It's a heartless betrayal to us all.'

Gertie Grimshaw was in her wheelchair parked beneath the umbrella of bare, bleached boughs and as Alicia stood chained against its trunk, Gertie began to lead 'We shall overcome', the beautiful protest anthem; young and old, rich, and poor joined in the singing in the most harmonious display of unity that the village had ever seen. The prickly divide between the original and newly settled villagers from Tiggy's growing-up days had healed, standing united in their common cause to save the Lightning Tree. The local press gathered with their cameras poised for action, expecting another great news story; Alicia's stunts were always media gold. The atmosphere was lively and buoyant: Glenda Harrington, Beryl, and Rach were handing around the flasks of coffee, biscuits, and cupcakes whilst they waited. It had the light-hearted energy of a charity coffee morning until workers in hard hats arrived. The threat to the tree suddenly seemed very real: the digger man was in his cab, and three workers on the ground put on their protective clothing, getting the ropes and chainsaw ready for action.

'Sing louder!' Alicia shouted to the protesters, making her presence known as she guarded the tree in her chains. 'Join hands, everyone, and make a circle around the tree!' she instructed.

'We're under orders,' a woman said, adjusting her hard hat, 'this ain't any of our doing.' They looked at each other, realising that their task wasn't going to be easy or without resistance.

'Nobody, move a hair!' Alicia yelled over the top of the singing. 'Hurry up, Hugo! You're meant to be getting the order quashed.'

Things were getting desperate and down to the wire as the workers started up the chainsaws, drowning out the singing. Arthur Ramsbottom could hardly bear to watch; the loss of his beloved tree was inevitable.

Hugo F. Uppingham had done his best to save the tree and to thwart the council's development plans. It had taken two arduous days of hearing all parties' points of view for the Inspector to make his decision.

The chainsaws were throbbing and the digger moved in closer. The tree's human chain broke into fragments as some of the ECM children backed away, covering their ears to block out the noise. Two of the younger children started to cry, unable to bear the sound of the saws. Alicia and Gertie held firm, guarding the tree as the digger moved in.

'We're here to stay!' Alicia shouted as both the photographer and digger eased closer. 'You don't scare us!'

'A bit ironic considering how scared she was of Simon for memorising his father's chainsaw manual!' Penelope whispered.

Suddenly, the press got what they hoped for as the diggers moved across a huge area of mud and puddles, spraying the dirty water over the two women.

The onlookers gasped but continued singing as Alicia had ordered.

'Good gracious!' Arthur mumbled, 'it couldn't happen to two nicer ladies!'

Alicia was shielding her eyes from the mud when Hugo Uppingham and a pin-stripe suited council official turned up in a Land Rover.

'Put down the saws! The Inspector has ruled for the tree to remain,' the council official announced through a loudspeaker. 'Plan aborted!'

The protesters cheered and hugged each other, forgetting that a very mud-splattered Alicia remained chained to the tree. Arthur burst into tears, completely overcome with joy. The Lightning Tree was safe, and there was also to be a preservation order.

'Nice work!' Arthur said, shaking Hugo's hand. 'I honestly can't thank you enough.'

'Mine's a double brandy!' Hugo said, patting Arthur on the back as everyone headed off to celebrate.

'Don't just leave me here! Is that all the thanks I get?' Alicia cried.

Daisy Dingles and 'Simple Simon' were the first to rescue her.

'What darlings you are!' Alicia said, giving them both a hug. 'I got you so wrong.' The local press had captured it all.

✿ ✿ ✿ ✿ ✿ ✿ ✿ ✿ ✿ ✿ ✿ ✿

A few weeks after the Lightning Tree received its preservation order there was more good news for the village: the new road and housing development would not be going ahead. It was business as usual at the track and Every Child Matters. Tiggy and Buddy wandered past the baseball field that hadn't seen any action since Todd's disappearance. The overgrown grass told the story of how long Todd had been gone; it needed cutting, but it didn't really matter now. Tiggy consoled herself that maybe it was all a bit too American for somewhere like Great Snubington as she tried to reason with the emptiness she felt. As usual, Solomon, loyal to his routine and habits, was sitting cross-legged in the batter's box, drawing in a world of his own, dealing with the loss of his friend in the only way he knew.

Since Todd had disappeared, Solomon would draw nobody or nothing other than Todd and sometimes his campervan. Tiggy expected today's sketch to be no different, but it was. Solomon had drawn the Lightning Tree bathed in sunlight on the surrounding landscape, and whilst Todd wasn't there, something else was, a rainbow in the sky and a baseball headed towards it. Solomon had never drawn anything like it before. Tiggy's eyes burned into the ball. It was undoubtedly Todd's face.

Solomon stared at Tiggy staring at his picture, stunned and silent until eventually she spoke,

'The Stig Man!' she murmured. 'You came to find me!'

Solomon nodded and clapped, and then, shaping his thumbs and index fingers to make a heart, he pointed to Todd's face on the ball and then to Tiggy, repeating it until she responded.

'Did Todd tell you that?' asked Tiggy, knowing that it was Solomon's love language.

Solomon nodded.

For a moment, Tiggy's heavy heart lightened, her shoulders tingled, and a warm sensation ran through her body. She hadn't had the feeling in a long time, but she recognised it instantly. Angel Seraphina was sending her a sign that all was well far beyond.

'I can wait,' Tiggy said, feeling the tenderness of Seraphina's message.

'Should we wait for Todd together?'

Solomon nodded, and his lips crinkled upwards. It was a small smile, but it was nevertheless a smile of approval.

Tiggy sighed. It had been just over a year since Todd had first appeared in the village. What a year it had been, but for now, she was back at square one, on her own again, but this time no longer looking for 'the one' to spend the rest of her life. She knew who he was and where he was. He just needed to come back to her. Only Todd's campervan and a few bits and bobs remained, including his red holdall. Solomon had found it and was 'looking after it' for Todd, using it, at Tiggy's suggestion, for his 'go everywhere' sketch pad and pens. She still had the four leafed clover paperweight in her care; it was like Todd's 'calling card' that she would treasure just as she always had the Stig Man's friendship stone; two different names she had shared two distinct and meaningful life chapters, but it was all with one person, one incredibly special person. Todd had unlocked her heart, locking his aura inside, and then, when he left, had thrown away the key; their instant connection and deep-rooted feelings from their unforgettable history were such a part of them both, it was present in every heartbeat. Tiggy knew that Todd was her soul mate, together or apart. She cupped the paperweight in her hand that she would keep next to the Stig Man's friendship stone now back on the mantelpiece and sighed, but then she smiled. Tiggy sighed because she missed him, but smiled with gratitude for having had Todd in her life again, making more memories to add to the last. At least Solomon understood, and now they would tackle their emptiness together.

'My dear Solomon,' she said philosophically, 'When life gives you lemons, make lemonade!'

ABOUT THE AUTHOR

Amanda Ryan is the author of 'The Indigo Trail', and 'Broken Angel' is the sequel.

Since writing her debut novel, life's events have made Amanda increasingly conscious of having many more roads in her rear view mirror than stretching ahead. Consequently, Amanda's love of travel and new experiences dominate her 'to do and wish lists', and she recently flew the 'Velocity' zip wire over the Penrhyn Quarry.

Amanda believes that we should always strive to carry on learning, pushing our boundaries to continue growing through life. Around every corner is somebody who can teach us something, and in fact, she says that the older she gets, the more she feels she still has to learn. Since her 30s, Amanda became increasingly aware of how we all think, feel and process information and experience the world around us so differently. She was wrong about things she held to be true, and recognising the richness of neurodiversity in its many colours and shades, she wanted to find out more. She considers that it has been a subject in the shadows for such a long time, directly affecting so many people; its ripples far-reaching, often unrecognised, misunderstood, and little talked about but crying out to be heard.

Nevertheless, Amanda has a far less serious side with a child-like sense of fun, her age just a number, never tiring of playing in the snow, blowing bubbles, and adding magical touches such as wizards and dragons to her 'Enchanted Garden'. She also loves mulled wine in winter, the scent of roses in summer, and making good memories amongst family because, as we all know, the little things really are the big things.

Amanda enjoys hearing from her readers and may be contacted at amandagreg6@aol.com

9 781805 418344